UNNATURAL DRAGONS

Published by Clockwork Dragon
www.clockworkdragon.net

First printing, June 2016

Unnatural Dragons is a work of fiction. Names, places, and incidents are either products of the authors' imaginations or used fictitiously. No endorsement of any kind should be inferred by existing locations or organizations used within it.

No dragons, werewolves, vampires, scientists, aliens, or AIs were harmed in the making of this book.

ISBN: 978-1-944334-10-9

a science fiction anthology

UNNATURAL DRAGONS

Clockwork
Dragon
Books

Dedication

For Connie...

...Lindsay's treasured friend.

...a weird old lady Jeff has noticed often shows up to events.

...Lee's second mom, a woman charming enough to think "Tolkien-esque" is a compliment.

....someone Sechin met once and shall always hope to meet again.

Editor's Note

Clockwork Dragon began as a partnership between Jeff and Lee. The pair found they enjoyed working conventions and events together and decided to make it a Thing. Jeff, as an author best known for his award-winning steampunk trilogy, Dawn of Steam, is the clockwork. Lee, someone obsessed with flying lizards, is the dragon.

Along the way, Jeff and Lee found other authors who share their goals, visions, and fondness for genre fiction. Together, Clockwork Dragon is a group of people dedicated to producing high-quality fantasy and science fiction and working together to help each other succeed.

This anthology came from our involvement in the Writerpunk Project, a group dedicated to supporting the PAWS no-kill animal shelter in Lynnwood, WA, through the organization and sales of anthologies.

As authors, we love to write, and realized the group needed something involving every member to make the group feel complete. Our name offered an obvious way to theme at least two anthologies: clockwork and dragon. But we couldn't do things the obvious, easy way.

Thus, we present a collection of science fiction stories about dragons. Within these pages, Lindsay takes us to a genetically engineered fantasy world. Jeff imagines a future where the machines rule. Lee revisits her Maze Beset trilogy to bring a new story about superheroes. Sechin reveals history from his Mad Science Institute trilogy.

Enjoy.

Table of Contents

The Dragon Within   1
    by Lindsay Schopfer

Angel Wing   47
    by Jeffrey Cook &
    Katherine Perkins

Alien Dragons   105
    by Lee French

The Chupacabra and the   161
    Dragon
    by Sechin Tower

Lindsay Schopfer is a writing coach and instructor for Adventures In Writing, where he helps writers learn about and improve their craft. His workshops and panels have been featured in a variety of Cons and writing conferences across the Pacific Northwest. He is also a mentor for Educurious, a Gates Foundation-funded program designed to connect high school students with professional writers.

The Dragon Within

LINDSAY SCHOPFER

Rick Tansom looked out the transparent walls of the space elevator at the vibrant green landscape and velvet purple sky. The lift descended gradually, giving him ample opportunity to admire the verdant forests bathed in the light of Wellia's four moons. None of the trees were natural, of course. The genetically modified oak and aspens had been test-marketed and engineered to serve the dual-purpose of serving as a living backdrop while maintaining the terraformed atmospheric changes necessary to keep Wellia's air not only breathable, but intoxicating. Rick wondered if perhaps there were chemicals mixed with the air to make the world feel magical. Probably.

Wellia was a fairy tale come true. A land of elves, dwarves, unicorns, griffins, talking trees, nymphs...all carefully created in a laboratory to synthesize an entire world of fantasy and magic. Someone pushed against him from behind to get a better view, and he moved aside as a man that seemed all eyebrows, nose, and beard muscled his way past to ogle the planet. Glancing around the crowded elevator, nearly all the tourists bore the marks of either cosmetic or surgical augmentations designed to make them appear more like the fantastic creatures that had been created for this world. Only Rick was not in costume.

Eventually the elevator came to a rest at the loading dock, and the willing herd of eager guests crushed toward the exit. Rick waited in the back of the group until the throng had mostly passed before leaving the elevator and emerging into the initial reception area. Despite the security checks they had already endured at the space station, Rick's group was divided into lines and slowly funneled through another series of checkpoints.

Like all of Wellia's employees, even the security guards were in costume. Each of them a reptilian schradin, the imposing security officers wore armor and carried spears that identified them as lizard-men warriors. Not the choice that Rick would have made for security officers, but it was an old and common mistake that companies made. Make the security scary, and people will stay in line. The problem with this tactic was that it made security unapproachable, and the vast majority of innocent tourists would be that much less likely to report suspicious behavior.

Eventually, Rick made it to the scanners. The schradin at his station glowered at him, but Rick regarded him coolly as he withdrew his badge from his pocket.

"Rick Tansom, Interstellar Security Consulting."

The schradin's eyes narrowed, but he nodded. "We were told you were coming, sir. May I scan your badge?"

"Of course."

It took three seconds for the scan to clear, and just a few more for Rick to pass through the rest of the checkpoint. While Rick was sure that the automatic sensors had detected the powerful firearm concealed under his jacket, the security guard merely waved him through. Moving through the terminal, he saw a young, elf-like woman standing with a sign bearing his name at the end of the runway. Unlike the various women on the elevator, this girl had more than the typical augmentations. In addition to the customary pointed ears, facial tattoos, and slight build, this girl's entire face had a sculpted grace that couldn't be inherited naturally. She wore a silky, flowing gown that revealed just enough of her body to suggest that she was lithe to the point of being almost avian-like, and she exuded a grace and austere magnetism that had every male human past puberty glancing her way. Even Rick had to admit that he felt a small amount of pride that she was waiting for him with a smile that she could have charged for.

"Mr. Tansom?"

Her voice sounded like the notes of a golden harp.

"That's me," said Rick.

"I'm so glad. My name is Elli'tara. I've been instructed to take you to our resort director as soon as you made landfall. May I take you there?"

"Please."

Rick followed the unearthly beauty through the terminal and into a long corridor that was more window than wall. Massive oaks towered above them, shading them from the vibrant twilight trickling through the transparent ceiling.

"Did you have a pleasant flight?"

Rick looked away from the gently moving leaves to Elli'tara who was somehow managing to gracefully walk forward while giving him her undivided attention. He looked into blue eyes decorated with fine runes around the irises and shrugged.

"It was fine. You people have quite a place here."

Elli'tara blushed and grinned like a schoolgirl with a crush. "You are so kind to say so. We do try so hard to make Wellia as close to a living dream as we can."

"Are you one of the administrators?"

"Me? Oh no." She gave a small musical laugh and placed a feather-light hand on his arm. "I'm simply a humble cast member, and today, I am your eager guide."

A cast member. It figured, though he would have

preferred to talk with someone who had some authority. They were interrupted by a young man with fake horns glued to his head and a suit of what looked like artificially-lightened chainmail. Years of training and experience had Rick analyzing the suddenly appearing man as a potential threat, and then just as quickly dismissing him. Even with the realistic swords on his hips, Rick was sure he could render the young man immobile, unconscious, or dead before he could draw them. It was all in the way he carried himself, not to mention the all-consuming look of desperate longing he was giving Elli'tara.

"Pardon me, my lady," he said, giving what he probably thought was an impressive bow. "Would a humble Arashic warrior be permitted a picture with thee?"

Elli'tara's glowing smile somehow became both warm and distant at the same time.

"I'm sorry, but I'm very busy right now. Later, I am sure."

They began walking again as the horned tourist followed them.

"But where will I find you?"

"I will be at the banquet at the Father Oak Hotel at nine tonight. I will be available then."

"Okay, it's a date!"

Elli'tara smiled as they left the horned tourist grinning like an idiot. Rick glanced back at him before turning to his guide.

"Do you get that often?"

"Of course. It's my primary purpose."

They were stopped several more times by eager tourists, all men, who wanted a picture with the elfin girl. Most were well-behaved and accepted her excused apologies, though one of them continued to follow them and even took hold of her hand. A schradin security guard immediately started coming toward them, but Rick had already reacted. He took the man's fleshy arm and pressed his index finger into a nerve just behind the elbow, his eyes hard as tacturian steel.

"The lady said no. Move along."

The man's eyes went wide as he whined and twisted, his fingers releasing Elli'tara's hand as his whole body contorted. Rick released the steady pressure and turned to continue walking with Elli'tara, leaving the tourist to nurse his numbed arm as the schradin had a quiet, firm conversation with him. Elli'tara blushed.

"I apologize for that," she said.

Rick shrugged. "It wasn't your fault."

Elli'tara led him to a special lift for staff members only, and soon they had emerged into yet another corridor. Rick immediately recognized the austere settings of a corporate business center, very different from the fanciful trappings found elsewhere in the resort. Aside from the breathtaking view out the windows and the tendency toward fanciful themes in the tasteful artwork, he could have been walking down the halls of any number of corporate buildings on any number of human-colonized worlds.

They soon came to a conference room with an open veranda that looked out at the silver moons just touching the crowns of the distant oak hybrids. Elli'tara gestured toward one of the dozen empty chairs around a swooping desk.

"Please take a seat. Yool-pik will be here shortly."

"Thank you."

Rick sat in the chair until Elli'tara had left, then immediately got up to walk out on the veranda. The view was breathtaking. A fading sunset painted the sky in great swathes of purple and green, highlighted by the gigantic silver moons that took up a full quarter of the sky. Off in the distance, Rick could see a single oak hybrid larger than all the rest lit up with the golden lights of towers and gazebos carved into its bark and branches. For a moment, Rick was reminded of a much more innocent time, when he would sit in bed listening in rapt attention as his mother read him fairy tales and the classics of Earth.

He was trying to remember the titles of each of the antique paper-and-ink books she would read from when he heard skittering footsteps behind him. Turning, he saw a pleudarkian in a flowing silk robe that complimented its variable skin tone, currently a soft, faded blue. Its sensory nodes bobbed in a friendly manner as it crossed the room and came out onto the veranda.

"Quite the view, isn't it?" said the creature, its 'voice' emitting from a tiny vocalizer device near its vestigial wings. "I'll often come out here and taste the colors when I'm not working."

"Yes, they're very nice."

"Allow me to introduce myself. I am Yool-pik, acting resort director. I believe you spoke with a representative of my employer, Mr. Carsawn. He's the one who felt we needed the services of a private security consultant."

"Rick Tansom," said Rick with a polite nod that served the purpose of a handshake with a creature that had no hands. "I did some research on your business and your daily operations, but I'd like some more details into these threats you've been receiving."

Yool-pik sighed, its side-gills vibrating slightly. "You must understand that we receive false threats regularly, just like any other major business. Of course, perhaps the specific nature of our resort draws a larger number of eclectic customers than usual."

"I noticed. One of them tried to run away with my guide on the way here. I practically had to peel the guy off of her."

"It's an occupational hazard for all of our cast members, and not to be unexpected. After all, we made sure each one of them was irresistible."

"So it's true, then? You really are genetically engineering cast members?"

Yool-pik's flesh flushed a dull crimson. "I didn't say that, Mr. Tansom. We are not breaking any of the laws of this system. That is all that you should need to know as a security consultant. Don't go poking your nose where it doesn't belong. I wouldn't want to have to file a complaint against you with the Cross-Galactic Confederation."

Rick's eyes hardened. "Let's understand something right up front, Yool-pik. I'm not some rent-a-cop so desperate for work that I'll tell you whatever you want to hear to get paid. I can get by just fine doing the work I want to. I can live very cheap if I have to, and if someone rubs me the wrong way, then I have to. Now, your Mr. Carsawn reported suspected terrorist activities, and I've got the experience and the skills to help keep your little fairy world running. I can even get my hands a little dirty when it comes to preventing serious damage. But to do that, I need to know everything I can about what kind of a facility you run and who might not like the way you do business. Was all that clear or should I say it again slower?"

Yool-pik's coloring went almost black. "I doubt you get much repeat business."

"Only with the people I want to. Now, suppose you give me a straight answer this time? Are you genetically engineering cast members?"

Yool-pik's coloring cooled to a navy blue. "The nature of our business requires extensive genetic engineering. Everything from the terraforming oaks to our fanciful animals are artificially created. As far as our cast members go, some of them are created in our labs, but each of them is given citizenship rights as members of the Wellia Colony. You can verify that with a simple background check of any one of them. You can also investigate their living conditions and treatment as much as you want. There are no violations of the rights of sentient life here. In fact, all of our genetically engineered cast members are virtually indistinguishable from our physiologically modified cast members. Even your guide this evening was one of them."

Rick thought of Elli'tara and had to admit he wasn't all that surprised. While it had been feasible that she had been born human and then physically altered later, the cost of such major surgery was probably prohibitive. Besides, there were some subtle things genetic engineering could accomplish that mere surgery could not, no matter how advanced.

"You mentioned fanciful creatures," he said. "Do you mean things like dragons and unicorns?"

"Unicorns are easy. We have a small herd that we use for mounted tours. But dragons are sadly just not possible. It's the fire-breathing, you understand. The flying is very difficult as well, considering the size of the creature that our guests would expect."

"That's gotta disappoint a lot of people. Maybe even make them angry enough to make some idle threats?"

"I told you," said Yool-pik, "we've had our share of empty threats and trolling. We would not have contracted your services for something that harmless."

"Do you know who it is that's making the threats?"

"Only by the name they give themselves, 'The Order of Darkest Light.' "

"Darkest light? What's that supposed to mean?"

"Who knows? We've heard much stranger pseudonyms concocted by our guests for the duration of their stay."

"Do you have any record of a guest or group of guests referring to this 'Order'?"

"No, though that's hardly uncommon."

"How did you receive the threats?"

"Through hacked guest accounts. The Order gains access to an account, writes their message, then moves on. They never use the same account twice."

"May I see some of these messages?"

"Of course." The pleudarkian entered a dozen commands into a small device built into the arm of its chair and a hidden hologram projector blazed into life in front of Rick. Yool-pik made another adjustment on the device and a message appeared in the image.

```
Wellia, your childish games
pale before the Darkest Light.
Prepare yourself.
```

"That was the first message we received," said Yool-pik.

Several more messages appeared, each one similar in tone and subject to the first.

"This is the latest one."

Rick read it aloud.

```
Play-kings of Wellia, you have
wasted the gifts given you.
Judgment comes.
```

"Any idea what might be meant by this statement about wasting the gifts given to you?"

Yool-pik waved a vestigial wing dismissively.

"It's a common complaint from our critics. They say that Wellia feels more like an amusement park than a true fantasy world. They'd like to see something more real."

"Like what?"

"Monster hunts, for one. They'd prefer it if we engineered creatures like ogres and goblins and then organized real hunts where guests would get to kill them. They also want to use state-of-the-art medical treatments to justify using real weapons on each other in the live-action roleplays."

"They sound pretty bloodthirsty."

"I suppose, though there are certainly those of our investors who would agree with them. Of course, we'd then have to deal with the engineered-lifeforms activists. There's no pleasing everyone, even on a fantasy world."

"Well, I can start with a full inspection of your current security system. We'll see how well you're equipped to handle a potential terrorist attack."

"You agree that they are terrorists, then?"

"Could be. Either way, I need to know what sort of precautions you have in place. I'd also like to check the Interstellar Enforcement Division's information channels for any other signs of the Order of Darkest Light. And my people will need access to all of the guest accounts that were hacked."

Yool-pik turned an acquiescing green. "Have your people contact me directly. I can put them in touch with my information overseer."

"Good. Now, if you don't mind, I'm awfully tired from the flight. Could we do the inspection in the morning?"

"Of course. A room has been prepared for you in the Castle of Hightower Hotel. It's the closest to our command center. I'll call a guide for you."

Rick had to admit that there was a small part of him that was disappointed that his guide was not Elli'tara.

Though the brunette host with clipped ears was easy on the eyes, she lacked the innate magnetism that Elli'tara seemed to possess without even trying. Rick suspected that Yool-pik had exaggerated when he said that guests couldn't tell the difference between those cast members who were simply augmented and those who had been specifically engineered by the company.

The Castle of Hightower Hotel was only a short tram ride away, though it was late enough that Rick could see little of the structure besides the colored fountains and splashes of light playing over its many towers. As the tram lifted up and over the outer wall, he spied what looked like a pitched battle being fought in the courtyard below. Remembering what Yool-pik had said about the demands for more violence from the Order of Darkest Light, he peered down to try and make out some details of the melee below him.

"It's a staged battled for hotel guests," offered the guide. "All of the hotels have several battles scheduled every day. In addition, each evening-battle always has a storyline associated with it."

"What kind of storyline?"

"That depends on the theme of the hotel. Here at Castle Hightower, it's a battle for the succession to the throne, with the winning 'monarch' getting to rule the castle the next day, making choices such as what sort of activities will be available and which dinner option the kitchen will prepare. At the Father Oak Hotel, the guests fight over the fate of the elven princess, who will either be sacrificed to a dragon or taken into hiding."

"A dragon? I thought you didn't have dragons on Wellia."

"It's a free-moving mechanical. Unfortunately, it's impossible to engineer living dragons at this time. Would you like to participate in one of the battles? I could add you to the signup list."

"I don't think so. Play-battles aren't my sort of thing."

Soon they were in the hotel and Rick's guide led him to his room. Stepping inside, he had to admit that the décor was a good mix of the fanciful and the functional. He particularly liked the tapestries, and was examining a scene of a knight and a dragon when his guide spoke up.

"Dinner's already been served, but room service will be open for another hour. You can order from the menu by the communicator. Is there anything else that you require?"

"I don't think so. Thank you."

The guide bowed and left. Rick went to the communicator and examined the menu. After a moment's consideration, he contacted the kitchen and ordered the Squire's Banquet. While he waited for his dinner, Rick punched in a series of commands on his wrist-unit to bring up a holographic interface in front of him. After checking his various message depositories and reviewing the security report of the home apartment that he saw more through a camera than with his own eyes, he dialed up the number of his informational assistant. After a brief wait, the projected face of a smiling female lukassian appeared before him.

"Good morning, Rick. How are things on the Fairytale Planet?"

Rick made a face. "Artificial. You wouldn't like it, Marvis."

"Maybe you should take me on that dream vacation you're always promising and let me judge for myself."

"And keep you from your work? I wouldn't do anything so terrible to you. Listen, I need you to do some digging for me on a possible terrorist group. Get in touch with Yool-pik. He's the resort director and should be able to get you the necessary access codes along with links to each of the accounts that this group has hacked to make their threats."

"Will do. What's this group call themselves?"

"The Order of Darkest Light."

Marvis made a face. "That's both over-the-top and nonsensical. Sounds like terrorists to me."

"I'll be sure to pass along your expert appraisal. Give me a ping when you find something."

"Shouldn't be too hard. I'll start with a broad

spectrum search on the alias, then start digging into the tracer code."

Rick's door chimed.

"That sounds great. I'm going to eat my dinner and go to bed."

Marvis smirked. "Good idea. You don't want to work yourself too hard. You might break a sweat if you're not careful."

"Goodnight Marvis."

"'Night Rick."

Cutting the connection, Rick answered his door and took the tray from the porter. The Squire's Banquet turned out to be bangers and mash with maloovian eggs and a sweet cream stew that came in a bowl that simply couldn't hold enough. After dinner, Rick removed his wrist-unit and got undressed.

Turning off the light and climbing into bed, his last two acts of the day were both motivated by experience in self-preservation. The first, hi-tech. He dialed the sensors in his wrist-unit to detect any kinetic, chemical, or thermal fluctuations beyond a certain threshold and respond with a corresponding alarm. The other precaution was as old as mankind. He slipped a weapon under his pillow, though he opted to forgo the traditional dagger for a PX-14 auto-repeater hand cannon. Thus prepared, Rick fell asleep to dream of dragons and castles for the first time since he was eleven years old.

Rick was dreaming of lizard-men and unicorns when a persistent ringing dragged him from slumber. Not really awake yet, he reached under his pillow and forced his senses into action. His room was still dark, though his movements had already activated the motion sensors and turned on the low-light illumination. The incessant electric tone kept playing, and for a moment he stared in confusion at his wrist device. It took him a moment more to wake up enough to realize that the persistent chirrup wasn't his alarm, but a simulated bird chirping somewhere in the apartment. He stumbled to his feet and activated the room's communications holograph. Yool-pik's three-dimensional image appeared, it's highly detailed face a little too clearly defined for that early in the morning.

"Hello?" said Rick.

"Tansom! You need to get down here right away. There's been an attack!"

"Where are you?"

"The security center. I'll send someone to get you."

Rick was just finishing getting dressed by the time

his door chimed and a schradin security officer stepped inside.

"Are you ready, sir?"

Rick nodded and followed the guard from his room and down the hall to the high-speed lift. Rather than going to the tram depot, the reptilian officer led him to a free-moving hovercraft outside the hotel.

"Can you tell me anything about the situation?" Rick asked as they sped through the night.

"Sorry sir, but I was called on duty after the event. All I know was that there was an attack at the Father Oak Hotel."

In a matter of minutes they had reached the resort's central hub and were hurrying through hallways to the planet's organizational center. After passing several security checkpoints, they emerged into a well-lit room full of furious activity as staff members rushed from one console to another, each one talking like he was the star of an action holo. Rick ignored them all and went straight to Yool-pik in in the room's center.

"What's the situation, Yool-pik?"

The pleudarkian turned to him, its obsidian-black skin shot through with pus-yellow streaks. "We've been attacked. It's the Order."

"Okay, one thing at a time. What kind of attack was this? Was there an explosive? Aerosol? How were you hit?"

"It was an assault team. They flew in on a private transport, made their attack, and left again."

"Casualties? Injuries?"

"Two security guards were killed when they tried to stop them. Fifteen cast members and guests were hurt in the attack. One is missing."

"The guard said that they hit the Father Oak Hotel. Did it seem like they had a specific agenda, or was it a random attack?"

"There was nothing random about it. They were all in character."

"What do you mean they were in character?"

"It was all captured on the security surveillance. You can see it for yourself." The pleudarkian waved a vestigial wing at a nearby security officer. "Chief Pelt, can you show Mr. Tansom the footage we have of the attack?"

The human chief of security led Rick to a nearby console.

"This footage was taken in the throne room at the Father Oak Hotel," he explained. "There was a live-action role-play in session at the time. I'll start it just before the attack."

Pelt called up the holo image of a room that looked more like an oversized gazebo than a throne room. Delicate arches and pillars shaped out of living wood supported the intricately decorated space with a massive nearby veranda showing a breathtaking view of Wellia's four moons. A variety of people in gauzy, pastel clothing were enacting some sort of scene together, though Rick had a hard time following the flowery language and convoluted names. He managed to piece together that there was some sort of argument over the fate of an elven princess, which explained all of the false ear-tips. He even recognized Elli'tara among the group, and wasn't surprised when someone revealed that she was playing the part of the royal bone-of-contention.

Suddenly, there was an explosion and a cloud of smoke and dust. The holo quickly adjusted the picture to filter out the blinding cover and showed half a dozen armed figures in fanciful costumes rushing in through the expanded hole they had blown in the veranda. Each of the invaders wielded some variation of medieval weapon along with heavy-impact pulse blasters that were clearly not period-appropriate. Ignoring the many people lying injured around them, they took up guarding positions as one of them began reciting what sounded like a prepared speech with the aid of an electronic amplifier in the corner of his mouth.

"Hear me, simple play-actors of Wellia! Too long have you sat and squandered this mighty world, playing at childish games with no consequences or true passion. We are the Order of Darkest Light, and we shall purge the charlatans and interlopers from this divinely appointed world. Our first act will be to teach you all a lesson of what a true adventure is."

The man turned and pointed at Elli'tara.

"We will take your elven princess!" he declared. "If you wish her returned, you must quest for her. You will be told where your quest may begin. I wish you—"

He was cut off as two security officers burst into the room. There was a brief firefight, but the officers both fell with only one casualty among the invaders. His moment ruined, the speaker grabbed Elli'tara by the arm and dragged her out onto the expanded veranda to the waiting transport hovering nearby. The rest of his compatriots followed, dragging their fallen comrade along with them. Rick turned away from the holo as the transport left the scene.

"Was the attack isolated to this single encounter?"

"Yes, it was just the one attack you saw."

"Was there anything else that was taken besides the one hostage?"

The security chief cleared his throat uncomfortably. "You'll need to talk with Yool-pik about that. I'm not cleared to share that information with you."

"Fine." Rick turned and walked back to Yool-pik who was trying to hold three conversations at once with two holos and an orderly.

"Was there anything else taken besides the hostage?"

Yool-pik turned toward Rick, seemed to consider a

moment, then waved a vestigial wing toward a nearby conference room. Rick followed without a word, waiting until the door had slid shut behind him before repeating his question. The pleudarkian's sigh seemed to shudder through its entire body.

"Do you recall the question you asked me in our first meeting? About our artificially created life forms?"

"You mean like the unicorns and other things?"

"Yes. You also asked me about dragons, and I told you that it was impossible for many reasons. Well, that wasn't entirely true. Dragons are the single-most requested creature from both guests and our investors. For that reason, our researchers have worked for years to solve the dragon problem. And recently, we think we may have finally created it. The DNA code for a real, flying, fire-breathing dragon."

"What's this got to do with the attack tonight?"

"Our head of research and genetics wanted to keep the code safe until we could show it to our investors and receive the necessary loans to begin production. He wanted to keep it safe, off the grid, where no one would ever find it. So, when one of our cloned staff members went in for a regular check-up, he imprinted the code somewhere inside the clone's body. Nobody would ever find it, and we could retrieve the information whenever we were ready for it."

Rick stared at the pleudarkian incredulously. "You

used a clone to store a recipe for making dragons? Do you realize how ridiculous that sounds?"

"Please Mr. Tansom, I'm in no mood for this sort of thing right now. The fact is that my resort's most valuable secret has just been stolen and I doubt we'll ever get it back."

Rick rubbed his eyes and took a deep breath.

"All right. Let's think this through. Do you think that the Order knows that Elli'tara has the dragon code inside of her?"

"I seriously doubt it. Knowing their tendency for self-aggrandizement, they likely couldn't have kept something like that a secret. No, I think that we are simply the victims of horribly bad luck in their choice of victim."

"I have a hard time believing that these guys just happened to take the one cast member that has a secret formula written somewhere inside of her."

The pleudarkian turned away, its skin a sudden crimson hue.

"I never said she was the only one."

Rick's mouth fell open. There was a long moment of silence.

"You people have more security problems than I thought."

There was a knock on the door. Yool-pik opened it to reveal Chief Pelt just outside.

"Sir, we've gotten a message from the Order.

They've revealed where they're taking the hostage."

"Where?"

"Vesra, in the Gollus system."

Yool-pik's crimson hue cooled to a sullen blue. "That will complicate things. Vesra is outside the jurisdiction of the Cross-Galactic Confederation. It would take multiple cycles before we could successfully lobby for a seizure operation." The pleudarkian turned to Rick. "Mr. Tansom, it looks like the nature of your employment has shifted from prevention to problem-solving."

Rick arched an eyebrow. "I hope you aren't planning on me trying to storm some crazies' castle in search of a princess."

"If this is a question of money, you will be well compensated."

"Well compensated? You better be willing to pay through the sensory node if you're going to ask me to go after those guys on my own."

The pleudarkian regarded him coolly. "How much?"

"Well, lemme see…" Rick considered. "For this sort of thing… twenty-four thousand upon delivery."

Chief Pelt blanched, and while the pleudarkian's coloring went cream-colored, Yool-pik answered softly.

"I suppose we could—"

"—with expenses," said Rick. "Otherwise, I'm going back to bed."

"They agreed to how much?" said Marvis's projection.

"Twenty-four large, with expenses, all upon delivery."

"Well, that sounds wonderful, provided that you live long enough to pay me."

"When have I ever left you hanging?"

"Do you want me to answer chronologically?"

"Right. I forget the downside of hiring from a species with perfect memory. It's just lucky for you that I can't do without you anymore."

Marvis smiled. "Could you ever?"

"Cute," said Rick as he made a minute adjustment to the drive flow of his ship before turning back to his information assistant's projected image. "So tell me what you've got on the Order of Darkest Light."

"You mean besides the fact that they have the silliest name in your spiral? They're very vocal, I'll give them that. They've been trolling in nearly every large fantasy-themed intraspace network group that there is."

"Do they seem to have a consistent theme? Any sort of agenda?"

"Mostly, they seem outraged at role-players that aren't 'legitimate' enough. They seem to think that holos, roleplays, and themed resorts like Wellia are only posing, and need to up their game. Make things more real."

"There's two dead security guards and plenty of injured people that think they're a little too real as it is. Any sign of activity from the group on Vesra?"

"That took a little digging, but I was able to track several of the less careful members to the planet. They're keeping together—"

"Let me guess, they're in a castle under a perpetually stormy sky."

Marvis gave Rick a smirk. "Actually, they seem to keep their headquarters on the move. They've got themselves a hover yacht and an escort of walker drones and mech-suits to keep off the pests."

"That'll make things interesting. Any ideas on how I'll storm a moving fortress surrounded by killer robots?"

"Perhaps you should have thought of that before you accepted the new job from Yool-pik."

"He used the magic word. Do you have any ideas or not?"

Marvis shrugged. "Well, you *are* going to a planet without any formal government or Confederacy association. I'm sure you could make some friends there."

"Is that a commentary on my friends?"

"Take it as you will."

"And how would I convince these new friends to attack an armed convoy?"

"The Order does have a very nice yacht."

Rick gave Marvis a sly smile. "You are a devious little angel, you know that?"

Marvis gave him an innocent look. "All I know is that you have the frequency of Elli'tara's tracking chip, so you can lead anyone you find straight to a large, shiny toy that a bunch of bad people don't really deserve."

"Thanks, Marvis."

"Just try not to still be on that yacht when the new owners take possession of it. They may just think you're one of the amenities."

Rick blew on his hands and rubbed them together, shivering despite the circulating heat of his thermal jacket. He moved slightly to try to find some position that didn't jab his sawed-off mine launcher into the small of his back. A small stone dislodged from under his boot and clattered down the canyon wall. Nearby, a nasty-looking tempaj rumbled and adjusted its elongated back limbs. Rick watched Neyat with detached caution. The tempaj looked up to meet his gaze with three saucer-sized globular eyes.

"You got a problem, farl?" he gargled.

"Just keeping an eye on you, Neyat. Don't want a sensitive soul like you to catch cold."

The tempaj's sickly tan body flushed a dull violet in mottled spots. Rick watched him coolly, adjusting the setting of the lerric gas rifle in his hands from "scatter" to "blast."

"Keep your skin pale," he said in a low voice. "Grinseng wouldn't want me to have to open up your ugly face and blow our cover."

Neyat opened his jaws to reveal his barbed tongue in a nasty snarl. A shift of pebbles signaled the approach of Logri, Grinseng's human lieutenant.

"What're you two multacks doing over here? Keep it down."

Rick sniffed, wiping his runny nose on his sleeve. "Just clearing something up with Neyat."

Logri glared at Rick with artificially colored lime-green eyes. "You just remember whose side you're on when the shooting starts, Tansom."

Rick returned the icy stare. "I'm on the girl's side, Logri, not yours. I agreed to help your little band take this convoy only so I could get to her. You just make sure none of your boys get any ideas when it's all over with."

Logri's reply was cut off by a crackle from the communicator hanging at his shoulder. A guttural language sounding like water rushing over the microphone followed, and Logri lifted the receiver to his lips in reply.

"Acknowledged. We'll be ready on this side."

The gargling voice replied then cut the signal. Logri lowered the receiver and scowled at Rick. "They're coming. Grinseng says to wait until the shooting starts and then move in. You'll have a few minutes before the fight's over to run in and grab the girl. Make sure that's all you take with you, and our men will be too busy looting the caravan to stop you. Understood?"

Rick nodded. "I understand. It's been a pleasure doing business with you."

Logri spat on the frozen ground. "Just make sure your back doesn't get in the way of one of my shots."

"Or mine, farl," Neyat said with a leer.

Rick pointedly ignored the tempaj and nodded to Logri as the man's communicator gurgled once more.

"They're coming," Logri said. "Get into position."

Rick turned and focused his attention on the dusty trail winding through the pass, keeping a weather eye on Neyat. The throaty roar of the convoy echoed among the canyon walls for a moment before the vehicles came into sight. Rick powered up his levboard, fitting his boots into their holsters until he felt the satisfying click of the locks.

He turned his rifle back to its "scatter" setting and crouched behind an outcropping, listening to the thunder of approaching machines.

The first of the vehicles rounded into sight and Rick grimaced at the sight of two automated assault runners moving side by side at the caravan's head. Like two black beetles, they scurried across the frozen ground, their turreted pulse cannons slowly spinning on their tracks. These were followed by three heavily armored troop transports rolling on wheels as tall as a full-grown human. Rick gritted his teeth as the next vehicle rumbled into view. A levitating land yacht painted in gaudy pinks and silver-whites floated like a flower surrounded by heavily armed thorns.

Suddenly the walls of the canyon exploded with the furious reports of the weapons of Grinseng's followers as they opened fire on the convoy. Rick flipped the switch to his magnetic repulsor shield and pushed the button that activated the secondary diffusion screen. A hazy blur surrounded him even as he tilted his right foot in its socket on the levboard, sending him bursting out of his hiding place at a blazing speed, his left foot aiming him toward the starboard side of the land yacht.

Almost instantly, he felt the slight jostling of bullets pushing and deflecting off of the magnetic field surrounding him. Surges of deadly energy dissipated harmlessly in the diffusion screen with fizzling crackles. A second blast of successive shots pounded his rear-facing shields from friendly fire. Or unfriendly fire. Neyat was just lucky Rick had something more important to worry about.

Up ahead, the three armored troop transports had stopped to disgorge their squads of mech-suited fighters as the land yacht picked up speed. The leading assault runners were also joined by two more coming up from behind, and together the four skittering vehicles pulled in close around the yacht, pummeling the canyon walls with their pulse cannons. Rick flew over the canyon floor, leaning hard to the left to dodge a barrage of shield-draining blasts from the foot soldiers. He left his lerric rifle on his back. It would be useless until he lowered his own shields.

Reaching the base of his target, he used a large boulder as an impromptu ramp to soar up above the hull of the land yacht and land squarely on the deck. Spotting an open hatchway, Rick dove down a well-lit staircase leading into the vessel. He pulled his rifle off his shoulder, checked to make sure he was alone in the hallway, and flipped off his shields.

Buzzers were sounding all along the corridor as a harsh voice made garbled announcements over a crackling sound system. Rick moved quickly through the hallways. All the doors were closed and sealed shut. The ship rocked from a large explosion somewhere toward its front. Rick had to hurry.

He turned a corner and nearly collided with a large pleudarkian holding a phase rifle in its tentacles. Rick drove his fist into one of the thing's mossy green nodes, knocking it to the deck with a liquid thud. He crouched down and placed the barrel of his rifle against one of the pleudarkian's pulsing sensory organs.

"Where's the elf girl?"

The pleudarkian spluttered and swallowed. "C deck," it gurgled, "down the stairs and on the left."

"Thanks."

With a sharp rap to the creature's central sensory node, the pleudarkian was out like a dead bulb and Rick was up and moving again. The deck shuddered as a thunderous explosion reverberated throughout the yacht. For a moment, Rick felt as if he were falling, then he slammed back down against the hard deck. The yacht's levitation engines had been hit. The vehicle was grounded. Rick nursed the levboard's throttle and made for the nearest stairway leading down. He had very little time left before Grinseng's gang would be swarming all over the vessel.

He sped down the stairs to C deck and stopped at the door the pleudarkian had directed him to. There was no guard outside the room, but he took no chances. He paused a few yards down the hall from the door and stepped off his levboard. Flipping his magnetic shield back on, he left the diffusion screen off to allow him to fire his own rifle. He took a quick breath, set his rifle to blast, and shot the closed door. The carved tolgron wood exploded in a shower of splinters immediately pierced by the burst of gunfire from inside the cabin. With a flying leap, Rick launched himself forward to land on the floor in front of the shattered door. He held his fire for half a breath to look inside the room.

A sturdy table had been knocked over to make a temporary barricade. Two reptilian schradins crouched behind it, blindly firing their powerful rifles at the space above Rick's head. A small figure crouched in the corner pressing her hands against her long, pointed ears. Rick aimed swiftly, blasting holes through table and schradin alike with two shots. Splinters rained in the small room as Rick quickly scrambled to his feet and hurried over to the huddled figure in the corner.

"Elli'tara? It's me, Rick Tansom."

The elven girl looked up, her tilted eyes melting from fear to overwhelming relief.

"Oh Mr. Tansom!" she exclaimed, leaping into Rick's arms. "I was so frightened!"

Rick was startled to find that she weighed practically nothing as she clung to him. He tried to ignore the sudden rush of emotions that came with holding the girl in his arms, forcing himself to remember that it was all a chemical response to specifically engineered character traits.

"Are you all right?" he managed to ask. "Did they hurt you?"

"No, they treated me very well. Like royalty. They only became angry whenever I stopped playing the part of a captured princess."

"Well, you're a rescued princess now. Mostly. We've still got to get out of here, and quickly. I had to make a temporary alliance with a local gang that will probably expire once the attack is over."

Elli'tara's angular eyes went wide.

"You came here alone?"

"I was in a hurry. My ship is on autopilot and should be able to pick us up once we're clear of the battle. Let's go."

Elli'tara nodded and allowed herself to be hoisted up onto Rick's back, pausing first to grab a nearby tapestry to protect herself from the hard edges of Rick's power pack. They left the room and Rick stepped into the waiting levboard, powered up both his shields, and accelerated toward the staircase. They had just begun to climb the stairs when the lights in the land yacht went out, surrounding them in inky blackness. Someone must have shot out the power supply.

Rick powered the levboard through the darkness as fast as he dared, using the low-light vision provided by his HUD visor. He turned the corner at the top of the stairs and saw the welcome shaft of daylight at the end of the hall leading to the deck. Suddenly the light was blocked by an enormous figure holding a smoking pulse-bomb launcher.

"Farl!" gurgled Neyat nastily. "Who's gonna save you now?"

Rick didn't hesitate as he gunned the levboard's throttle. The board surged forward, roaring down the narrow corridor with a humming whine. Rick twisted his front ankle and drove the leading edge of his board into Neyat's shocked face even as the tempaj fired off a wild shot with his bomb launcher that missed Elli'tara's pointed left ear by mere inches. The levboard launched Rick and Elli'tara up into open daylight. They sailed in a wide arch up and over the rail of the yacht as Neyat's poorly aimed bomb detonated in the hatchway behind them. The levboard came down hard on the ground and gripped earth, hurtling Rick and Elli'tara at breakneck speed along the canyon floor and away from the dying vessel.

A nearby explosion sent the levboard skidding sideways and Rick had to struggle to keep himself upright. He risked a look behind him. One of the Order's automated assault runners had broken off from the main conflict and was skittering at an alarming pace toward them. Rick floored the throttle, swerving randomly from side to side to throw off the runner's aim. He glanced up at the sky for any sign of his ship, but found only a partashi sky fighter strafing the yacht's ground troops.

The assault runner was falling behind them as its insectoid legs struggled to keep pace with the levboard's superior propulsion. Rick risked another look over his shoulder and relaxed slightly as the beetle-like machine retracted its grenade launchers in a vain attempt to increase its speed. He waited until the large barrels disappeared into the runner's armored shell before yelling over the wind to Elli'tara.

"I'm going to lower the shields so I can signal my ship!"

Elli'tara tightened her grip around his neck and nodded. After a quick glance at the assault runner behind them, Rick flipped off the shields and activated his communicator, signaling his ship to approach from the south-west, away from the battle.

"It should be here in just a few minutes," he called over his shoulder as he powered the shields back up.

"Are we safe now?"

Rick glanced back at the pursuing assault runner. The drone's legs blurred as it attempted to maintain its pursuit, but the powerful levboard was increasing the distance between them by the second. Rick gave a short sigh of relief.

"I think so. We'll just need to—"

"Look out!"

Rick swerved to the left more out of surprise from

Elli'tara's sudden scream directly into his ear than from any meditated maneuver. A concussive blast rocked them like a small boat on a stormy sea as the diffusion screen around them sizzled angrily. A look to the sky dragged a groan from Rick as he saw the partashi sky fighter flying low enough above them to make the pilot visible. The creature flying the one-person fighter was a black and orange stripped krenlin with a flared crest pulsing with quivering fury. It was Grinseng.

An amplified translator attached to the fighter rang through the canyon walls. "Tansom! The deal has changed. Hand over the girl. She must worth something if you want her so much!"

Rick cursed his bad luck. Grinseng had all the advantages. While his ship would be arriving in minutes, without him to operate it, the craft would be next to useless in a firefight with the heavily armed sky fighter. Rick's mind raced as he tried to come up with a plan. Another explosion tore at the ground just yards away.

"You will stop!" roared Grinseng's translator. "I'd rather not damage the girl, but I'll blow you both to bits if you do not stop now!"

Rick ignored the warning and tried to remember the specs on a partashi sky fighter. One pilot, low atmosphere flight only, armed with explosive pulse cannons and charged recoilers. A light design gave it greater maneuverability but weakened hull strength.

Protected by a magnetic field, diffusion screen, reverse force buffer...

Rick grinned. A reverse force buffer protected against nonmetallic projectiles using the same technology that kept his levboard a foot above the canyon floor. It was effective at long distance, but at close range a powerful shot could penetrate it. His lerric gas rifle wouldn't be strong enough to break through, but he knew what would be.

"Take this," he called back to Elli'tara, handing her his rifle. He reached back to the small of his back and removed a sawed-off delayed mine launcher. He watched Grinseng's fighter circling around for another pass. The krenlin lined up his fighter and dropped into the canyon, his wings dipping below the canyon rim as he sped toward them from behind.

"Hold on!" Rick shouted to Elli'tara as he whipped the levboard around to speed back toward the approaching sky fighter.

Grinseng peppered the frozen earth ahead of them with blasts from his heavy cannon as they rapidly approached each other. Rick waited a moment more, then floored the throttle of the levboard and twisted to place the reverse-force buffer directly against the nearby wall of the canyon. With a sickening lurch, the levboard shot up the side of the sheer cliff, climbing laboriously toward the canyon rim. Grinseng's fire stopped abruptly as Rick and

Elli'tara drew within a dozen yards from him. Too late, the krenlin seemed to see Rick's plan and tried to pull up above the canyon. Rick quickly aimed the mine launcher for the fighter's intake vent and fired. Four of the green pulsing mines stuck together in a close formation even as the levboard stalled in its upward climb and they began to fall.

Rick's stomach seemed to float up to his throat as the ground rushed up to them. Tucking the launcher under one arm, he quickly punched the levboard controls on his wrist, cranking the reverse-force buffer to maximum intensity. They crashed back down to earth with a rattling impact, the bottom of the levboard almost scraping the ground as the device fought against the pull of gravity. Rick managed to wrestle control of the levboard back and looked up at Grinseng's sky fighter. The delayed mines' timer ran in the upper corner of his vision. 5…4…3…2…

A horrendous explosion tore the sky open above them. Rick swerved to dodge the large chunks of flaming metal as the shields around them fizzled with the smaller debris of Grinseng and his fighter. A predatory grin split Rick's face as he lowered his shields and contacted his ship again. Soon, the reassuring silhouette of a sloop class starship crested the canyon rim and lowered itself toward them. Rick steered the levboard up the opened ramp. Elli'tara released herself from his back as he quickly ordered the ship to ascend to orbit. Rick powered down the levboard and stepped onto the deck of his ship, feeling the surge of power as the craft lifted itself up and away from the cold ground and the firefight still going on behind them.

Rick went to a nearby porthole and watched the canyon he had sped through only moments before grow tiny and disappear into the broad expanse of a continent shrouded in clouds. In less than a minute, the curve of the horizon was visible, and then the planet itself began to fade into the sea of stars. At last, he breathed a sigh of relief.

"We're safe now. Are you all right?"

"Yes, thank you," said Elli'tara, her voice still a little shaky. "Thank you for coming for me."

"Well, I was in the neighborhood. I hope you can find some way to make yourself comfortable for the flight back to Wellia. There's only one chair, and I need that to drive."

It was early evening again on Wellia. Rick stood at the open balcony of his room and watched the four moons slowly rising on the horizon. He wondered if the day would soon come that guests would watch the silhouettes of dragons across those distant moons. Would Yool-pik and the owners allow the dragons to fly free? Would they remain caged like animals in a zoo? He was still pondering when the door to his room chimed.

"Come in."

Rick was a little surprised when Elli'tara entered his room. She looked like she had already completely recovered from her experience on Vesra, giving him a smile that was an exact duplicate of the one she'd given him when they'd first met.

"Good evening, Mr. Tansom. Yool-pik sent me to let you know that your payment has been processed, including your expenses."

"Thank you. Marvis will be happy to hear that, though I'm sure we'd have noticed the large deposit in our account without anyone telling us about it."

Elli'tara's porcelain cheeks showed a hint of rose as she replied.

"Actually, I was wondering if you were planning on staying on Wellia for a time. There'll be a wizard's festival in just two days at the Apprentice's University. We have short-lived nanite injections that would allow you to cast real spells."

"No thanks. I'm actually leaving in the morning."

"Oh, I see. Then I suppose I will wish you a

pleasant trip then. Unless I can convince you to come to the elvish banquet we're having tonight? Due to the damage to the Father Oak Hotel, we've scripted a special crossover event with the Underground Dwarven Kingdom."

"I've already eaten. Thanks all the same."

Elli'tara nodded and turned to go. Rick hesitated a moment, then called out to her.

"Actually, I did have one thing I've been wanting to ask you."

The elf-girl turned.

"Yes?"

"Did you know that your creators were storing the secret of creating dragons inside of your body?"

To Rick's surprise, she smiled.

"Of course. I had to give my consent, after all. I do have citizen's rights on Wellia."

"So you've known all this time?" Rick shook his head. "I'm not sure that I'd enjoy serving as someone's memory storage device."

"I suppose if you think of it that way, it might feel like a violation of some kind. But that's not how I thought of it. Consider, Mr. Tansom. How many people can say that they truly have a dragon inside them?"

Rick smiled. "I suppose you're right. Good night, Elli'tara."

"Goodbye, Mr. Tansom."

She left, and the door closed behind her. Rick turned and looked out at the moons, imagining Elli'tara's children winging their way through Wellia's night sky.

Jeffrey Cook lives in Maple Valley, WA, with his wife and three large dogs. He was born in Boulder, Colorado, but has lived all over the United States. He's contributed to a number of role-playing game books for Deep7 Press out of Seattle, Washington, but the Dawn of Steam series are his first novels. When not reading, researching or writing, Jeffrey enjoys role-playing games and watching football.

Angel Wing

JEFFREY COOK & KATHERINE PERKINS

Mari pressed as tight as possible to her dragon's back, the wind loud in her ears. It wasn't loud enough to cover the grinding sound of the massive arms of the giant city mecha behind her. When those sounds lessened, Mari knew who was buying them time. She tried not to think about it as she held on, as Talaitha flew with all the speed she could manage. It was their job to survive.

Behind them, Talaitha's sisters and their riders died.

"To Joan and Baroness!" Three glasses of what

passed for beer these days clinked together. Three dragons made a long, low sound. The survivors of Angel Wing had all been cleared for duty, and final memorials were simple.

In this case, they stood in a field near the former Bassano Dam—long since just scraps and rubble along the river, its power generator torn apart to keep it from the enemy—for one drink. Soon there'd be word about how the intel raid had gone, and the squad would probably be back in the air within the week.

Luxury was a thing of the Old Days. Now, the machines owned their cities. Humans hid where they could. The land that was once the Siksika Nation Reserve was as good a place to do so as any, but the people who'd come there to coordinate against the Calgary AI did much more than hide.

Which was why they had more funerals.

"Joan was always so welcoming, from the start," Kirsty said. "I can't help but wonder if she and Baroness would have been safer if there'd been a real rider watching out for them."

"She was welcoming because you were welcome. And Kirsty, cut it out," DJ said. "They had a real rider watching out for them. And Rachel and I weren't exactly chopped liver handling our ends either. We were all doing our jobs, but war is war, and we're only flesh and blood. That being part of the war."

"You never let me get away with anything," Kirsty

said, smiling thinly.

"Darn right. Especially not buying into any B.S. about whether you're real. There's 1400 pounds of very real fire-breathing dragon—even with a silly name—saying otherwise."

Kirsty's exasperation was comfortable. "All those clicks and rasps and THRUMMs—it sounded right when I hadn't met any yet!" She'd named Deathwhistle before finding out that most who had been properly recruited and trained in the program gave their dragons names like Lucy or Betty or, of course, Ada and Charlene.

All conversation stopped, however, at the sound of a glass clinking, set on one of the rocks that were strewn about the field. DJ and Kirsty turned. Rachel Yellowbird was stroking Ada's arched gray back and cupping her own ear, with its fitted piece of dragonbone, listening to a sound her squadmates couldn't hear. The dragons were listening, however, and all very agitated.

"Is it a call for help?" Kirsty finally asked. She'd never been fitted for an earpiece—and that wasn't something, for once, that she could blame herself for. They were rare, one per squad, and Lt. Yellowbird was the most qualified. Rachel had worked in computing before she entered the Dragonbound Project. For some time, she had run the punched cards from one clacker to another, analyzing the little codes and reprocessing them elsewhere, fulfilling the duties done by various circuits, busbars, and routers in the Old Days, before such things turned traitor. Before that, Rachel had in fact worked with the not-yet-nightmare machines themselves, when computing was a very different thing. At any rate, all that analytic experience had given Rachel the knack for picking up on the dragons' unique method of communication. She'd been recruited and, as Ada was engineered, trained to receive and relay squad communications, since electronics were too easy for the machines to track.

Rachel shook her head in response to Kirsty's question. "More like 'in case I die before I get there,' " she said. "A speed-drake coming back alone via the usual re-directs. The raid was a disaster."

"But was it a failure?" DJ asked, his voice all Squad Leader now. He moved from dragon to dragon, including his own immense Charlene, settling all of them. He'd been in rodeo before the Digital Treason and all its accompanying disasters, and afterward, among the refugees who'd filtered in from all over Alberta and parts of the Northern United States, he'd been one of the most natural dragon-wranglers even before he'd been provided his own. The dragons quieted down, but still seemed at attention as all the humans looked at the communications specialist.

"Nope," Rachel said. "They've got the plans."

Kirsty approached the computing room just as Rachel was coming out of it. Through the doorway, she could see the mass of people turning the handles of the analytical engines, talking as best they could over the clack-clack-clacks of the turning cylinders and cogs, the slamming of inked metal slowly against paper.

"How's it coming?" Kirsty asked. She had no idea what the clackers would have to do, with jury-rigged light sensors and conversion wires, to extract the plans from the datadisk, but they'd all been on overload since the survivor of the raid had been brought in.

"Bit by bit," Rachel said. "Almost literally. I'm out for a while. Want to check on Ada."

"DJ's been keeping a good eye on her."

"I know he has. How're the patients?"

"Both recovering well, the medics and the vets say. Physically, anyway. Do you know Mari?"

"Mari Thuleja. 23. Speed-drake named Talaitha. No, I don't know her."

"What kind of name is Talaitha, anyway?"

"An actual name." Rachel smiled thin. "Unlike some."

Kirsty smiled back. "Fine." Her face slowly fell. "I don't know how to say this…"

"It's okay. Just say it."

"Back in Bozeman, we kept busy, but … it's so hard here. In the time it takes to say good-bye to the dead, half a dozen more have joined them. Literally. And I know we can't slow down because *it* won't slow down, but—"

"—but we're not it," Rachel said. "That's part of the point of…everything. Calgary apportions its energy and presses forth its automata. We can't do that. We're only flesh and blood. It's what we've got. All of us, even our biggest 'weapons.' Our own flesh and blood. It goes in the vats for a reason, beyond just the hemo-imprintation bio-babble from Bozeman."

"Hey, we managed some pretty impressive bio-babble. And yes, I know, we're not unstoppable hunks of metal, and we're all family, and you and DJ don't care, and Joan didn't, that I'm only in this family because of a lab accident…"

Rachel rolled her eyes. "Every single human being left alive is family, as far as I'm concerned. But I think you and Deathwhistle are a lot more than an accident."

Kirsty smiled warmly, but then it fell again. "I can't stop thinking about Joan."

"It still wasn't your fault."

"I don't care. You think that girl in the infirmary, after running out on her squad, cares if she did everything just right?"

"That's the trouble, I guess," Rachel said. "Brains are just flesh and blood, too."

When Kirsty and Rachel arrived at the pens, DJ was playing with Charlene, going through some of their 'games' to help teach her different battle commands. Deathwhistle and Ada were occasionally joining in. Midway through a sonar test game, Ada stopped the sonar clicks, and looked toward the exit to the base, clawing at the dirt. Charlene and Deathwhistle soon did the same.

"Family call?" DJ asked. He couldn't hear anything, but he'd known them long enough to guess well. The Angel Wing clutch, raised together, had certain unique signals for communicating with each other.

Rachel's hand cupped her earpiece. "Yes, but there's something more. Can't quite get it yet."

DJ had long since learned to trust her when Charlene started getting agitated, so by the time the runners showed up, he was getting Charlene saddled and ready to fly.

"Incoming, incoming!" the first runner shouted.

"Seekers?" he asked the young man, grabbing the

messenger by the arm.

"Bigger, a lot bigger. They're saying mecha."

"But…" Kirsty looked around. "But how?"

"Maybe they keep some kind of trackers in their datadisks," the runner said. "Maybe they sensed something when all the clackers were cranked at once. I don't know."

DJ sighed, but nodded. "Those plans have already cost too many lives. They'd better be worth it."

Kirsty crawled onto Deathwhistle, talking herself quietly through the series of buckles and straps. No matter how many times she did it, it just never seemed to become a habit the way DJ and Rachel made it look. "Ready."

DJ took the lead, Charlene breaking up the wind resistance for the other two as they moved into a V pattern, one dragon short of the usual squad diamond. While dragons had many commonalities, different breeds had been tinkered by the lab techs in the deep gene-labs in Bozeman, Montana, designed to make a compatible flight. Angel Wing now lacked a speed-drake. Charlene, the biggest and the strongest flier, was a breakerdrake, designed to lead from the front and ease the wind for smaller dragons. Ada was a shriekerdrake, engineered to have an even wider vocal range—both for the calls and the standard sonic attacks—than her close cousins, as well as an enlarged audial plate.

Deathwhistle's breed was newer—and incredibly

necessary. The fire breath had taken a lot longer to figure out, and the firedrakes came with their own set of problems, but they also made more ambitious plans and assaults possible. The people who'd initially conceived of them had, of course, envisioned fire-breathing dragons as the new assault specialists, which sometimes worked fine against the fragile drones. The giant mechas that formed the centerpiece of the rogue AI's armies were too heavily armored, though, as the first, tragic raids discovered. Fire breath would never fare as well against mechas as the weaponized sonics—at which the firedrakes were the weakest, making Deathwhistle's name even more ironic. The real value of the firedrakes was messing with the AI mechas' sensors.

As they got into position in the air, Kirsty noticed those taking flight behind them. While four other assault wings were circling with them, a dozen speed-drakes were headed south, flying low. Messengers, in case the Siksika base didn't survive the night. The reasons that thought made Kirsty's stomach cold went far beyond the possibility of dying herself. Without the baseful of dragons to curtail the Calgary AI's drone excursions, the research center in Bozeman wouldn't be safe.

They didn't have to wait long. Even over the rush of air, they could hear the thunderous footsteps of the giant mecha and see the base shaking. The mechas were the AIs' terror forces, and they did that job well. Their energy requirements were enough to keep them at rest, on defense near most major cities, but when the AI did locate human bases, the giants had proved to be the most effective weapons. Long before the AI rebellion, humans had built plenty of missile shelters and the like, to guard against aerial assault. Nothing protected people from the giants digging out the entire shelters, or just collapsing them on top of the assault survivors.

"Get ready, fliers incoming!" DJ called, hearing the communication trills from his dragon shift to the sonar clicking. The rest of his squad would be doing the same. The air filled with explosions of fire, from the firedrakes as well as incendiaries and sensor bafflers going off from the base.

Missiles exploded around them from the incoming fighter jets. One dragon dove back for base, too badly injured in the assault to stay airborne, while another just fell from the sky under a more direct hit. For the rest, the mock targets and sensor interference worked, missiles exploding nearby, but not on target, or flew off-target entirely. A few others hit the base, destroying one of the gun stations before it got to fire off a shot.

Kirsty tried to stay focused on her own contributions to the fire-cover. She tried not to think about the casualties. Dragons healed fast, but some damage was faster. Baroness hadn't even been up against a mecha's entourage when she went down.

The jets slowed to dogfighting speeds, engaging the dragons in the air. Two exploded under assault from the anti-aircraft guns below as the wings got some ground support, while the dragons rose, spun, and dove, pitting their maneuverability and sonic arsenal against the raw speed and firepower of the jets.

"Charlene, play tag," DJ called, getting a response trill. His big dragon rose, making a target of herself, before diving. He knew the risks, and suspected the dragon had some idea too, but it remained one of her favorite games. They drew a triad of fliers. When Charlene dove, two missiles and a hail of gunfire missed the dragon by less than a foot, and the three jets shifted to dive after her.

"Suckers," DJ said.

He got Charlene to flatten out, streaking ahead of the gunfire as she led the triad into the firing arc of the anti-aircraft guns. Three bright explosions filled the skies behind him, and he circled back around to rejoin his wing.

They lost two more dragons in the skirmishing, as well as another gun, but they'd blunted the initial assault before they got a free run at the base. Just as DJ was doing a flyover and thumbs up for the gun crew who'd taken the triad off his tail, a section of the surface the size of half a city block exploded, taking two gun crews with it. The mecha was in range.

Charlene struggled to stay airborne against the shockwave, but managed. There were several seconds of confusion while dragons reoriented themselves, the massive blast interfering with their sensitive hearing—and with it, their navigation. Two landed rather than risk their dragons crashing, while others pulled up into holding patterns, circling while their mounts recovered.

"Char, trust me." She wouldn't be able to hear him, but DJ stroked her scales, trying to get the idea across anyway. When he rapped his right foot against her side, she turned to that direction, trusting in his navigation even if she was effectively flying blind. The other two dragons caught sight of their big sister and moved into formation to follow.

DJ led them toward the mecha, banking left to avoid a missile. At another signal, the dragons swept ahead of them with offensive sonics. Two more explosions ahead of him told him they'd successfully shot down a couple of the mecha's heavy missiles. He gave Rachel a nod, and the squad spurred their dragons on faster.

"Let's see if we're lucky," he muttered, hoping to get an attack in on the missile bays before the mecha closed them off.

They weren't lucky. Nevertheless, their assault forced it to close the missile bays, reducing the amount of firepower leveled at the base.

Two more fighter drones circled around it, providing cover and air support. Kirsty had to stay focused. The air filled with flame to their right and left, diverting the drones' heat-seeking missiles and throwing other IR and UV sensors and fire-control off target. DJ kept his attention on the drones, taking down one and going into dogfighting mode with the other, trusting Kirsty to guard the rear, making sure the dragons were never the hottest targets in the air.

Rachel made the first run at the mecha itself. She picked up altitude, then dove. Ada flattened her wings to her sides, and Rachel huddled in close to the dragon, diving at the mecha and narrowly avoiding an attempt by the giant to grab the dragon out of the air. As she dove along the body, the dragon probed the mecha with sonic bursts here and there. Rachel's earpiece picked up the chirps and clicks of the responses. Ada extended her wings again, picking up just short of the ground, turning the speed boost from the dive into forward momentum, racing along the ground and then rising just ahead of a heavy stomp from the giant. Through the adrenaline-fueled excitement of pulling off the risky scouting run, Rachel still had to give DJ a thumbs down. They hadn't found any structural weaknesses. At least she was able to come up under one of the drones, letting Ada sweep upward and tear a wing off as she passed. Ada then dropped the heavy debris.

"Char, Fetch!" As she swept past her, Charlene grabbed the wing from the air, clutching it close as DJ engaged another drone in a high speed game of chicken.

Instead of diving, he had Charlene flare her wings, catching an updraft and rising suddenly, while she dropped the debris. The drone exploded in a collision with the torn-off wing. With the skies near them temporarily clear of drones, Angel Wing closed in to make a full-squad run at the giant.

Charlene banked hard as a fist came at them, chirping a warning. The others followed suit, flying along the robotic arm, staying close to prevent the giant from using any of its ranged weapons. As they swept up along the elbow, the dragons opened fire on the joint, sonic blasts on different frequencies hitting the more lightly armored moving parts. As the mecha reacted, swinging that arm around, the dragons scattered, narrowly avoiding the attack.

"Stay tight, stay tight!" DJ shouted, trying to be heard over the battle, with Charlene clicking away, signaling the other dragons back to her. Ada picked up on it, and Rachel and her dragon passed on more commands, guiding the flight back into a V formation, staying in close to the mecha's body.

A hand closed just behind Deathwhistle's tail, the dragon lashing it out of the way at the last moment. DJ waved, and the rest followed around one of the mecha's sides before climbing. As the mecha turned, trying to locate the smaller targets again, DJ led a diving assault on one knee. The flight scattered again when the mecha brought a foot up to try to dash them to the ground.

This time, the giant was able to track them, opening fire on Deathwhistle. Kirsty spurred her dragon on, rushing ahead of the line of gunfire that tore up the ground behind her.

Seeing Kirsty drawing fire, DJ pointed upward and led a new attack, with Rachel trailing behind on Ada. Deathwhistle lit up the skies, trying to disguise DJ and Rachel's assault. Both dragons flew close to the giant mecha's body, clicking off sonar signals to be ready for any defensive movement. By the time the mecha noticed them, it was too late. They launched their assault on the head. Even there, the armor was too heavy to do any real damage, but the intense sonics at close range hit something in the giant's sensor arrays and were rewarded with sparks and smoke from the left side of the head.

They turned and dove away, Charlene getting clipped with laser fire from the defense systems in the head, losing control of her flight for a moment, but recovering before she hit the ground.

Aside from the defensive fire, the mecha stopped moving, trying to reorient itself after the sensor damage. Moments later, more trills and clicks filled the air, as the other squads caught up, bombarding the giant with a barrage of sonic firepower, while the trailing firedrakes filled the air with bursts of fire.

Under the heavy assault, the mecha fired, but hit

nothing, unable to lock on to any targets. Another squad's assault run focused in on the smoking section of the head, and this time, there was an explosion under the armor. The giant teetered, then fell forward to one knee. It was just starting to rise again when the next salvo of heavy fire came from the base.

By the time Angel Wing made another pass, the mecha's chest was damaged, exposing a critical weakness. Charlene led the squad through a rapid assault, all of the dragons hitting the damaged section with the sonic cries. There were more explosions as missiles exploded in their bays. The dragons stayed in tight formation, flying just over the mecha's shoulder, as the explosions set off a chain reaction, and the giant self-destructed from within.

Others celebrated as the mecha fell, but DJ glanced at his squad, shaking his head and turning for a run back to base as quickly as they could manage to get Charlene's injury checked, and to see if the clackers had made any progress with the data.

The map-turned-blueprint on the wall was made of half a dozen different sections of paper which had been sketched on for whatever fleeting moment the line data for that section had been available from the clackers. All had been taped together to show the layout of different systems within Calgary.

"We've been going over the stolen information," General Demian was saying. "And we believe we've found a vulnerable point."

DJ glanced at Kirsty and Rachel, not able to make much sense of the map beyond verifying that it did match his memories of Calgary.

Kirsty was busy scanning the map and didn't notice the glance.

Rachel spoke up. "The marked points are awfully deep into Calgary. Right past the city defense mecha, the air force that'll start scrambling on detection, and much of the city's embedded defense net. This had better be quite a weak point, General."

A couple of dozen riders nodded in agreement, but stopped when the general turned away from the papers and narrowed his eyes.

"Yellowbird, let me be clear. No one is happy about what has been lost here. No one is complacent about what has to be done, either. But it does have to be done. We have been exposed. Even if it was, in fact, in the course of getting the information, we have very little alternative but to act on the information before Calgary moves again. Understood?"

Rachel nodded.

The general resumed. "The data brought back indicate that there's a central server, here." He pointed to one of the red circles. "We've located as many other sensitive locations as possible, and we'll be staging attack runs on them to hide our primary agenda. As noted, the central server is near the middle of the city, but knocking it out should shut down the AI, including all defenses."

One of the senior base commanders spoke up. "So, we run a distraction, and send a commando team in to blow up the server?"

The general shook his head. "That was our initial thought, too. But the chances of successful infiltration without detection is essentially zero. Speed is our best weapon."

Kirsty looked up from the plans. "Looking at the map, that seems sound. Which speed-drakes do you have on the attack run?"

"You mean who would be insane enough," Rachel remarked under her breath.

"We'll need a full squad. Fire for sensor baffling, heavier sonic firepower to take drones and gunnery stations out along the path, and, as noted, a speed-drake for the necessary speed and agility to outmaneuver defenses for the final run at the servers."

The commander spoke again, clearly irritated. "Any obvious threat in the air that close to Calgary will draw a lot of firepower. The city also has multiple defense mechas. I don't see how they have a chance."

The general gestured along the streets and alleys of the map. "Based on the disasters on the east coast, we don't think the additional mechas will leave their posts until one sustains significant damage. In terms of your first point, the squad will fly low, use the city for cover. "

"Awfully narrow in spots there. You'd need some good fliers to make it," DJ said, looking more closely at the map.

"Agreed. These blueprints indicate the brain. We'll be needing Angel Wing to do the lobotomy. It will take two passes—one to drop explosives into the vent shaft to take out the grating, fans, everything in the way, and then a follow-up to blow up the brain."

DJ shook his head. "We don't have a full squad, sir."

"You do now," the general said. "Mari Thuleja will be joining you. She's the only one who has seen that far into the city's defense net firsthand, and I've been assured that she and her dragon are combat-ready."

"Combat ready, on a dragon ours have never worked with," DJ muttered. Out loud, he answered, "Yes sir."

After the meeting, a hesitant Mari joined them outside the briefing room. "I'm sorry, guys. It wasn't my idea."

DJ shook his head. "Nothing for it. Let's get the dragons better acquainted."

Mari provided an initial presence for Talaitha, then let DJ take over a lot of the handling. He directed the dragons, still on the ground, into a diamond formation, while Rachel stood, cupping her ear and making notes. Mari finally made her way over to Kirsty to chat. She wasn't feeling very good at it.

"I'm sorry about Joan and Baroness. I know you guys had been together a while."

Kirsty nodded. "I'm sorry about the rest of your squad. I can't even imagine."

"Thanks. They were brave people."

"Obviously, with what they did and all. We're going to make sure it wasn't for nothing."

"I appreciate that. I know they would too. Do you ever get nervous before a mission?"

Kirsty smiled faintly. "All the time. Every time, really. How about you? Are you okay to go back into Calgary, after…?"

Mari sighed. "I'm not afraid of the mecha, weird as that sounds. I'm afraid of the squad relying on me for the bombing run. The target for the explosives is tiny. We were infiltrators and scouts. Not an assault squad. I just don't want to get anyone else killed."

They sat for a while in silence, except for the sound of DJ's commands to Charlene, and the reactions of the respective dragons.

"I don't think Talaitha's going to learn to do tricks."

"Don't worry," Kirsty said. "She doesn't need to. They're just trying to get the hang of coordinating. Charlene's the only 'rodeo dragon.' Joan used to say that DJ —" She cut herself off and paused. "Um, well, the gist was, he's still a cowboy." She looked at Mari. "What did you do, before you signed up?"

Mari shrugged. "Whatever Dad needed done around the caravan, mostly. I was barely a teenager in the Old Days, and after the AIs turned, it was mostly a matter of finding here. You?"

"I was a researcher at Bozeman, back when this was all just a crazy controversial project that no one knew would end up a matter of life and death. Worked with the bone marrow samples. Then during the heavy times for dragon production there, until Deathwhistle was born, I was practically a glorified phlebotomist, finding veins and jabbing them."

"Good a job as any."

"Yeah, and I was good at it. To be clear, the accident that got my DNA in the dragonblood soup was not entirely my fault."

"So you didn't set out to be a rider?"

"Some days I still don't believe I am one. I should be working with the geneticists, but Deathwhistle hatched ready to bond with me, and she did. And she's part of one of the most successful clutches yet."

Mari sighed. "Which Talaitha isn't."

Kirsty winced. "Not what I was going for."

"Well, now I'm unsure whether I should worry more about people being uncomfortable that I'm replacing Joan, or whether I'm encroaching on your misfit turf. I'm not trying to out-I-don't-belong-here you." Mari forced a smile.

Kirsty snorted. "When you get down to it, I guess nobody belongs here. I mean…look at here. Last stand of humanity and all. Not exactly a place for shoulds."

"You were should-ing not three minutes ago."

"Yes, but I don't want you getting all that 'should' on you. You're the guest."

"Which is still part of the problem."

"…Granted. But if anyone can get the dragons working as a squad in the…not very much time we have, it's DJ. And Rachel practically speaks dragon."

An hour later, Talaitha was curled up between Charlene and Deathwhistle as Ada kept clicking and thrumming away.

"What's going on?" Kirsty asked.

Rachel raised a hand to her earpiece. "They're trying to work out a few modulations to the family calls, to make sure Talaitha can hear."

While she was explaining, Kirsty put an arm around Mari. DJ followed suit. "Welcome to Angel Wing," he said. "At least for the time being."

The squads hugged the ground to avoid detection for as long as possible as they approached Calgary.

The city sprawled to the greatest degree allowed by the two rivers. The outskirts of the city with the smaller buildings were still in the process of being converted—the old stone half torn down to be replaced by sterile expanses of metal and dark plastic. Further into the city, the AI's conversion was more complete, with the clusters of skyscrapers converted into the high-tech, towering edifices that the AI was originally designed to help oversee. Only the massive stadium grounds at one edge of the city remained visually similar to its origins, aside from the greater militarization that came with its current function as an air base, complete with its own guardian mecha.

"And we're here to kill it," Kirsty muttered as she took in the sight, the words in the wind lost from anyone else. The cities seized by AIs had been nightmares for so long. The idea they that were going to destroy a mind like that was still unreal.

Two other squads led the way for Angel Wing to draw the initial attention off of them. A dozen other squads split up, spreading out as missiles filled the air, coming right at the dragons. The two squads leading Angel Wing in stayed with them, while every other dragon and rider from the base that could still fly filled the air and engaged the city defenses or the mecha, trying to draw attention off of the attack run.

"Follow the leader, Char," DJ said, leaning against his dragon's back. Deathwhistle stayed low, in formation, while the other firedrakes with them left long trails of fire above them before diving to rejoin the squad. Shockwaves from the missiles exploding above nearly drove them into the ground not far below, and the heat washed over them. Angel Wing stayed in diamond formation behind Charlene while she flew right on the trail of the dragons ahead of her.

They emerged from the smoke and fire with the mecha looming. Above them, other squads were rising to engage the city's air forces, while others attacked the mecha, trying to draw its focus. The squads leading them in started attack runs on the giant robot, and DJ encouraged Charlene to bank to the left, staying tight to the giant's legs to try to draw as little attention as possible as they darted for the city streets.

Mari, trailing the rest of the squad to save Talaitha's energy for the bursts of speed to come, looked back over her shoulder. At first, she thought they'd evaded notice, until she saw three drones break off from the dogfighting in the skies to follow them into Calgary. She tapped a signal on Talaitha's neck, and the dragon warbled a warning call.

At the warning, DJ led the squad into an alleyway as the drones shot up the street behind them. Charlene and Ada exchanged a series of clicks and whistles as DJ zig-zagged through the city, turning into one alley and side-street after another, trying to prevent the drones from getting a clear line of fire. At a warning call from Ada, Charlene banked out of the way of a rocket from above. Lighter fire grazed her hide, thankfully doing minimal damage.

DJ glanced up, seeing a number of smaller hunter-killer robots atop the roofs, aiming down at the squad. He kicked Charlene's flank with his left foot, and she angled upward, then doubled back. A sonic burst sent the hunter-killer robots flying. Briefly rising above the rooftops, he saw dozens more swarming to firing points along the way. More drones were sweeping over the city, searching for them, and he was sure yet more were setting traps in the alleyways, if they took a wrong turn.

Charlene caught up with the squad, leading them around another corner just as more drones were catching up.

"Run and gun, Char," he called. Charlene clicked at the rest of the squad, and Ada sped up to come alongside her big sister. Talaitha in turn pulled even with

Deathwhistle, who turned her head downward, leaving a trail of fire behind them to confuse sensors as the drones came into sight behind them again.

Charlene and Ada took a hard left into an alley, blasting in front of them. The sonic blasts hit the drones trying to trap them, and both riders ducked low and shielded their eyes to avoid shrapnel. They took another hard turn, then another, trying to avoid being pinned down.

"THRRUMM!" Ada blasted snipers off the roof. But the drones still followed.

Charlene trilled. Ada took the lead as DJ gestured the squad ahead. Mari tensed. Charlene caught the lead drone with a blast, but the other two banked away from the explosion. Then Rachel led the squad around a corner, out of sight of the dogfighting.

Mari hunched lower in the saddle for speed—and to force herself to look forward as Rachel and Ada led them into another alleyway, leaving DJ and Charlene. Mari knew they were drawing drone attention, trying to avoid being cornered while more closed in from above.

More clicks and whistles. More sniper fire. "THRUMM!" More drones. Trying to lose them, Rachel led the group through three more turns in rapid succession, before finally leading them into the city center.

Several drones circled the area, and immediately turned toward them. Deathwhistle exhaled a particularly intense fire burst, drawing most of the drones toward the heat. Two of the drones, however, picked up on the movement, breaking off from their groups to pursue the dragons.

Kirsty didn't quite respond in time to the shots, and Deathwhistle's shoulder was clipped by an attack. The dragon managed to stay airborne, but her flight became unsteady. Ada dove in to attack one drone, sonic bursts destroying a weapon array and blowing up the flier. The other remained focused on Talaitha while the dragon zig-zagged right and left, avoiding fire, but making the attack run more difficult. Mari finally broke off, turning sharply to try to lose the drone and head back for the squad. By the time she reached them, more of the drones were breaking away from the decoy.

At a signal from Rachel, Kirsty guided Deathwhistle upward, the dragon turning in a shaky spiral, breathing a steady stream of flame. Some of the drones followed, firing all the way. Kirsty struggled to hold on as Deathwhistle struggled to hold the pattern and stay aloft amid the explosions around them.

Rachel charged the drone still on Talaitha's tail. It was too close for a sonic burst, so Rachel urged full speed instead, going for one of the melee attacks she usually preferred to leave to Charlene. Ada tore into the drone, causing its shots at Talaitha to go wide, before Ada raked with her back talons as well, finally destroying the drone.

After the dragon dropped the wreckage, Rachel cued Ada to call for Talaitha to follow close.

The communications specialist led the attack run, her dragon clearing the path with sonic bursts. As soon as the path ahead was clear for Mari, Rachel tapped on Ada's shoulder, and the dragon went into a wingover, turning suddenly and sharply to charge the drones breaking away from the firedrake to follow them instead.

Free and clear for the moment, Mari gave Talaitha a kick, and the speed-drake rocketed ahead. The dragon emitted two bursts of its own, destroying a few of the hunter robots that tried to form up on the ground below. Mari reached into her pack, drawing out the first explosives. She dropped those into the shaft and sped past.

Fire shot out of the vent shaft as the explosives went off, throwing up shrapnel. As soon as she could, Mari turned about, seeing both of the pairs with her locked in desperate battles with drones. She resisted the urge to help as she readied Talaitha for her next pass.

Fortunately, shortly after the explosions, the drones attacking the dragons peeled away. Unfortunately, all of the drones shifted their attention on the area around the vent, cutting off Mari's approach. She managed to urge Talaitha to rise in time, avoiding their attacks, but the drones had obviously gotten new orders, once the AI sensed its vulnerability. She sped back toward the others in her squad, Ada destroying one of the drones as it was trying to home in on the speed-drake. A look around confirmed that more drones were on their way.

Mari looked back and shook her head. Rachel nodded her understanding.

Kirsty rejoined them, Deathwhistle obviously struggling to stay airborne, and her puffs of fire were less intense. Still, she did her best to draw fire away from the others. She didn't want to fall, but she didn't want to let people down again, however arguable it was that she'd done it before. The stakes were too high.

Rachel gestured to Mari's pack and held out a hand. Mari nodded, going for her second explosive, handing it off as the dragons passed close, though she couldn't see how Ada was going to get close. Rachel tapped her dragon, and Ada gave off a complex set of signals. Talaitha and Deathwhistle formed up, the firedrake spitting small bursts of fire to draw off precise aim, as Talaitha responded by starting a new attack run. The drones, after the last attack, responded quickly.

Rachel undid the security straps on her saddle as Ada dropped low, then she dropped out of the saddle, rolling as she hit the ground. The dragons continued to draw fire, but intentionally focused on blasting the new hunter robots emerging into the area, even if the drones posed greater risks to the dragons, as Rachel ran toward the vent.

Rachel didn't see the drone missile explode behind

her. She just felt the shockwave throwing her forward and the burst of heat sear her back and shoulders as she curled around the pack protectively. She skidded along the metal ground, then had to spend a moment throwing up and recovering her sense of direction. As the stars cleared from her eyes, she pushed to her feet and stumbled the last several feet into throwing range. She primed the bomb and threw it into the vent before running the other direction as best she could.

As the explosion went up behind her, a scarred and burned Ada swept her up, carrying her rider away from the new explosion and the drone attacks. Several of the drones crashed into the walls of buildings around them, and more simply hit the ground, skidding to a halt, mostly undamaged, but also unmoving.

On the nearest rooftop, they watched the city of Calgary go dim, the lights going out starting from the center of the city and radiating out.

The faint crash of more falling drones in the distance eventually stopped. The thunder of mecha weapons stopped. Countless sounds of an automated city stopped.

Rachel just breathed heavily for a few minutes, still recovering her sense of balance.

Mari had already dismounted and was fretting over Talaitha. "Thank goodness they heal so relatively fast," she said between little reassuring words in the Romany she'd been raised with and subsequently raised the dragon.

"Definitely." Kirsty likewise braced and petted and soothed Deathwhistle. She reflected for a moment, then giggled nervously. She hoped she wasn't on the verge of some sort of relief-hysterics. "Listening to the lab staff argue at all hours about cell regeneration and insufficient examples of gigantotherm metabolism was more than worth it."

"Yeah," Rachel said absently, looking around.

Kirsty and Mari followed her gaze, stomachs tensing up yet again.

And like something out of the final scene of an action movie, DJ and Charlene arrived from the fight to draw off attention. Both had a number of new wounds from the battle, but nothing severe enough to keep them out of the air.

"I was looking for what seems like the heroines of the hour. Besides Charlene, of course," he said.

There were relieved hugs, Mari included. Kirsty and Mari then smiled at Rachel—who still was looking around absently.

"What's wrong? We all made it." Obviously, the others were a concern, but the squad was together.

"Can't shake something," Rachel said.

"Not supposed to shake combat adrenaline easily," DJ said as he stepped over.

"No… no, it's more than that. Do you remember ever being unnerved by the sound of an empty room?"

"I had three sisters," Mari said. "I don't think I ever heard any empty room." She kept trying to soothe Talaitha.

"We've got a lot of injuries to treat," DJ said. "And survivors to round up. We don't really have time to worry about it getting too quiet—Char, what's wrong, girl?" He looked over all the dragons. "They're antsy, not taking advantage of it like they should. Is Ada trying to convey anything, Rachel?"

"No, she's just not calming down, and I just… I hear something," Rachel said.

And then, for one moment, they all did. A tone. A cool, clinical reboot tone. And then the buzzing hum that had been just under the surface of conscious notice became louder. And the thunder of faraway mecha weapons began to reach their ears, along with the whir of drones taking flight. The city was awake.

"We've got to go," DJ said, looking at the lights coming back up. "They'll have hunters up here in no time."

"Did the bombs miss?" Mari asked.

Rachel shook her head. "I don't think so. I just don't think it needs one, central brain as much as everyone thought. All of the other computers around the city are picking up where the main server left off."

"So, what do we do?" Kirsty asked.

"Mount up," DJ said. "We need to get out of the city. Collect anyone we can and get out of here." He pulled himself onto Charlene's back, and the squad dove off of the rooftop and into the alleyways again.

It didn't take as long as DJ had hoped before they picked up trailing drones and hunters opened fire on them from above.

They turned through a couple of alleyways before a shot hit Kirsty in the shoulder. She screamed and sat up straight in the saddle, clutching at her shoulder. Deathwhistle slowed, trying to determine what was wrong. When a trio of drones came around the corner, Deathwhistle fired off a burst of flame to draw fire, but couldn't bank away from it fast enough.

"Run!" Kirsty had just enough time to shout, Deathwhistle echoing the call to her siblings to keep flying, before the shockwaves from the exploding missiles hit, sending Deathwhistle crashing into a skyscraper's exterior wall.

She managed to dig her claws in enough to slow her fall, but not arrest it entirely. Deathwhistle hit the ground heavily, managing to right herself enough to shield Kirsty from the fall. The dragon was still moving, but a wing was obviously broken, and she was favoring one front leg. The drones ignored them, pursuing the still-moving dragons.

"Well, Deathwhistle, what do you think? Is going down like that better or worse than it looks from up there?" Kirsty asked, giggling nervously. "Probably have fewer nightmares from it. For one thing, might be less time for nightmares. But we weren't…" She took a breath. "We weren't expecting to be immortal. Not like Calgary apparently is."

Helping her dragon as best she could, Kirsty glanced at the damage they'd done to the wall, noticing pulses of light behind one damaged panel.

"Deathwhistle, help me here," she said, guiding the dragon through tearing the panel free. Power conduits and indicators lined the surface under the panel. Tearing a couple more of them free revealed similar structures, with power flowing out to the city. She compared the different indicators and sensors, then led the limping dragon further in the direction the power was flowing from.

"Of course! Deathwhistle, destroy this." The dragon melted the conduits, and Kirsty had to dive away as the section went up in a small electrical explosion. "Okay, maybe that wasn't the best idea."

Despite her comment, part of one of the buildings went dark. Kirsty grinned. "Okay, maybe it was a great idea. Now let's…" She looked in the direction her squad had gone. "Let's do what we can here," she said with a sigh.

The drones may have ignored her. The hunter robots weren't about to do the same. Deathwhistle heard them before Kirsty did and dove into the way as the shots started. Kirsty went for her sidearm, knowing it wouldn't do much good. She braced herself behind the dragon and fired anyway, even while she heard more movement down a nearby alleyway.

"It's okay, Deathwhistle. We did everything we could."

She fired again, and three of the hunter robots exploded. Kirsty glanced curiously at her gun. Then two more of the robots blew apart, as the rest of Angel Wing swept in above her. As another hunter group emerged from an alleyway, Charlene dropped the section of a drone she was carrying, sending the piece of vehicle flying into the robots. While DJ and Mari swept the area for more attackers, Rachel landed next to her.

"There's fewer drones now," Rachel said, "but the city is repairing them as fast as it can. We have a path cleared for you, but you need to—"

"No, no, I need to explain. This is important. If we have even a few seconds, I need you to double check something for me."

Rachel relayed the message through Ada, and Kirsty pointed out the power relays and exposed indicators under the damaged section of wall.

The former computer tech looked it over, doing some analysis of her own. When the sweep was finished, the other two joined them.

"We don't have much time. There'll be more coming," DJ said.

"I thought I told you guys to keep going," Kirsty said. Before DJ had a chance to respond, she smiled and continued. "I'm glad you didn't, though. The brain is decentralized, but the heart isn't. I think we've found the blood supply—and an educated guesses where it leads to."

DJ blinked. "One more time?"

"Power lines," Rachel said. "It's consistent, most of the power for the city, maybe all of it, is coming from a main source. I think we've got a pretty good idea where it is."

"And that would be?" DJ asked.

"Under the stadium somewhere," Kirsty said. She'd found the vein. Now they had to do more than jab it.

Rachel looked at Mari. "How many bombs do you have left?"

"Three," Mari said.

Kirsty looked between the others. "We have some other problems, though. According to the intelligence, there's a mecha stationed right there, and there'll be drones. The stadium doubles as an airfield now. I know there's less of them, but…"

"But it will be a major fight to buy some time, yeah," DJ agreed. "Under the stadium will probably be swarming with hunters, too. Or it will be once there's an intrusion."

"That's just the beginning," Kirsty said. "The dragons won't really fit down there."

"Talaitha and I will fit just fine, and she's the fastest anyway, flying or running," Mari said.

Kirsty nodded. "All right, so we buy you time. We also don't have a map. No one charted down there."

DJ grinned. "The stadium? I spent plenty of time down there in the rodeo days. I'm sure it will have changed some, but I bet a lot is still the same. All right, here's the plan…"

DJ and Rachel drew the attention of the first drone patrols, goading them into following toward some of the higher buildings, where the dragons' maneuverability would be of more benefit than the straight-line speed of the drones. That thinned the air forces enough for Mari and Talaitha to start their own sweep, clearing hunter robots off rooftops in Kirsty and Deathwhistle's path. The latter pair were still critical to DJ's plan, but without being able to fly, and with the firedrake left badly in need of food and rest before her fire would be up to standards, they needed the help getting into position.

Kirsty did her best to keep the damage minimal, to try to not alert too many hunters, but she occasionally had to check the power lines leading out from the stadium. She had Deathwhistle heat up a building-side to soften the metal or melt a couple bolts, and then peel the metal back by claw.

Finally, she found what she was looking for. Deathwhistle tore up a portion of the street, exposing the juncture where numerous lines branched off to different points in the city. Kirsty got as much distance as Deathwhistle's short range would allow, and then had the dragon breathe a steady stream of fire, before pulling away as soon as the wire casings melted and the lines showed the first signs of bursting into flame.

They'd barely gotten into an alleyway when the explosion hit, setting off a series of other small explosions and fires under the street. Then a larger flame shot up like a signal—a signal she hoped might draw some additional help, if others had managed to destroy the mecha guarding the original entrance to the city. If not, it would still take attention off of the other dragons on their approach.

Mari and Talaitha waited after the sweep for hunters, with the speed-drake's claws dug into the side of a building, letting the dragon rest, hanging in place. When Charlene and Ada streaked by overhead, zig-zagging and weaving around buildings to avoid drone fire, Mari signaled her dragon to take off. She started off slowly, giving a wide berth to the electrical fire that Deathwhistle had managed to start, as it drew in drones and robot crews.

As soon the giant stadium mecha raised an arm to fire at Charlene, giving her and Ada its full attention, Mari urged Talaitha to greater speed. She evaded the attention of the drones all the way to the stadium's outer walls. The dragon hugged the wall, circling the building until she found what she was looking for: giant loading doors.

Talaitha stopped, clinging to the wall above her to stand guard as Mari rigged the first of the explosives. She knew that the doors being blown open would set off alarms, and after this, their best chance was speed.

The locks blew, and with a little help from dragon claws, the doors opened. There was no room for extended wings, but she could still ride, and Talaitha could still run. The pair disappeared into the dark, following DJ's best descriptions of his memories of the Stampede Grandstand.

"Fly circles, Char." The dragon banked right, evading the first blast from the stadium mecha. With the cover of the city and no expectations of coming under attack until the explosion hit, the mecha didn't even try to open its missile bays. That limited its firepower, but also kept it from presenting a potential vulnerability. Charlene launched a couple of sonic attacks anyway before diving. The already-injured dragons barely avoided a swung fist, staying close to the giant's arm, flying along its shoulder, and circling around its back. True to DJ's expectations, the drones ceased firing their heavier weapons, but didn't hesitate with lighter fire, the shots pinging harmlessly off of the giant's armor, and not quite as harmlessly off Ada's hide.

Under DJ's direction, instead of moving away, Charlene focused on using the giant body as an obstacle the drones had to chase her around, and on keeping the mecha occupied, circling between its legs, along the arms, and around and around the body, blasting as she went. Ada returned fire on the drones, given the opportunity, but most of the dragon's calls just kept Charlene coordinated on locations and numbers of incoming attackers. They were definitely doing their jobs and drawing attention.

To keep more machines occupied, Kirsty and Deathwhistle set two more junction fires. Kirsty didn't manage to get out of sight fast enough on the third. Deathwhistle managed to get in the way, taking multiple rounds from a hunter before they could get to the cover of an alleyway.

Kirsty pulled herself into the saddle, wincing in sympathy as the rider added more stress to Deathwhistle's injured leg, but the dragon bore it without complaint. Even her limping was faster than the human could have run, and this allowed them to use walls and rooftops for climbing and changing direction as she tried to avoid being located again. She did her best to angle herself toward the sounds of fighting near the original entryway to the city, hoping to signal help.

They came under more fire crossing a rooftop. Deathwhistle spun and breathed fire as Kirsty ducked low in the saddle, trying to make a small target of herself. The first two robots partially melted. Three others continued firing. She imagined she could almost hear them signaling and calling for aid.

Kirsty urged Deathwhistle to charge, hoping to shut them down so she could disappear again. The robots kept firing, dealing the dragon more wounds to the shoulder and chest before Deathwhistle reached them, tearing one robot in half and knocking a second off the building. The third was faster, and though its aim was thrown off, it managed to grab Kirsty's leg. She cried out as metallic fingers closed, and she thought she felt something break before Deathwhistle managed to bite its head off.

Decapitation, though it stopped further action, didn't do anything to alleviate the grip on Kirsty's leg.

"Okay..." she said hoarsely, still trying to recover her breath from the pain. "This is a bit of an issue."

She looked down. "Deathwhistle, we can't take a whole robo-corpse with us. I need you to help me get rid of it before the adrenaline wears off." Even with it, she was pretty sure this was going to hurt. Her courage worked up, she moved.

It was definitely a struggle, but Kirsty managed to get out of the saddle enough to let Deathwhistle get a better angle.

"Okay, Deathwhistle." She pointed just past the robot's wrist. "Sic 'em!"

Kirsty immediately sank her teeth into her off-sleeve to keep from screaming as the dragon bit the metal arm apart. This turned out to be an incredibly useful measure, and the sleeve stayed in place until Deathwhistle's gnawing and Kirsty's muffled keening were finished.

"Okay...okay. Good girl. And...and now let's just think of that hand as a leg brace, because it's going to take an industrial workshop to get it off. Time to get back in position."

She did, gasping.

"Okay, good job, Deathwhistle. Let's move before more show up."

Mari and Talaitha took one turn after another through the halls, hiding briefly in a storage area before a patrol passed. She ambushed two guardian robots at another set of doors, with an old sign indicating a staff-only stairway. She had hoped to finish them off with a blitz attack before they could send a warning signal, but with their thick armor—and Talaitha's claws designed more for traction and climbing than for attacking—she wasn't at all sure that was successful. She had Talaitha tear the doors open rather than wait on setting explosives, but had to get out of the saddle to lead the speed-drake down the steps and into the deeper reaches of the stadium.

The sound of masses of metallic footsteps echoing behind her told her that she probably hadn't, in fact, prevented the warning, but at least she wasn't hearing similar noise ahead of her yet.

She reached the bottom of the stairs, and then found another set of doors, leading deeper still. This time, disabling the alert guards took longer, and Talaitha was left with a deep wound in one shoulder. Mari did her best to quickly stop the bleeding, but didn't have time to tend it properly.

"I'm going to try to avoid any pseudo-poetic comments about blood on my hands," she muttered, looking at the mess from what little she was able to do for Talaitha. "I'd end up in an angst-off." The dragon kept following, occasionally turning back to look in the direction of the noises behind them.

Upon reaching the bottom of the next set of stairs, they circled. A steady hum grew louder and louder as they moved. Finally, Mari stopped on seeing two larger security robots bearing heavy weapons, guarding a heavy security door. The hum was louder here, drowning out all other noises.

With that distraction drowning out the metallic footfalls, and focus ahead, Mari missed the patrol coming up behind her. Talaitha didn't, pushing her behind cover as shots riddled the hallway. Peeking out from cover, Mari saw both hulking guardians go on alert, turning her direction and leveling their guns.

The drones were closing in too fast. All the zigzagging along the stadium mecha's broad chest helped them avoid fire, but also cut down on their speed.

"Off the wall, Char," DJ called, hoping Charlene's trill would warn Ada. The big dragon kicked at the mecha's chest, leaving shallow claw marks in the heavy armor as she pushed off, the maneuver letting her change direction swiftly. Charlene blasted one of the drones, which careened out of control, crashing into the mecha's side. Ada didn't push off hard enough and barely managed to twist out of a direct collision with a drone buzzing by her. With Rachel's guidance, the dragon grabbed on to the drone instead, powerful wings trying to turn it.

Unfortunately, the mecha didn't seem to be under the same restrictions as the drones. While they didn't fire their heavier weapons where it might hit the giant, the mecha didn't hesitate. It swung a massive hand at Ada. The dragon and rider managed to spin upside down, presenting the drone as a shield. Even with the flier serving to block part of the impact, they were still hammered downward, hitting the ground and rolling.

"RACHEL!" But DJ couldn't spare the time to see if they were still moving, having to immediately engage in a dogfight with another locked-in triad of drones. He guided Charlene around the mecha's side, while repeat fire raked along the heavy armor just behind him. "We can't stop, Char. They won't."

Kirsty reached the outskirts of the city, seeing the remnants of the fight. The city mecha was still fighting, but was firing blindly, its head and primary sensors showing heavy damage.

A few dogfights still raged around it, while bodies of dragons and drones alike littered the battlefield. Watching for several seconds, unsure what to do, she finally risked drawing attention from inside the city to try to draw some attention from outside of it. "Deathwhistle, flare."

The exhausted dragon took a deep breath and launched three quick bursts of flame high into the sky. She was quite sure that it wasn't accidental that one of them hit one of the drones. It wasn't enough to take it out of the sky, but the combination of heated metal and damage apparently overcame whatever systems they had to prevent the drones from targeting one another, and friendly fire in the form of a missile finished it off.

She heard the sound of metal behind her, and Deathwhistle spun. Kirsty felt her leg jarred as a shot hit the metallic arm clinging to her leg, and another shot grazed her thigh. Deathwhistle returned fire, but even on a direct hit, the partially melted lead hunter kept coming, as another took aim with a rocket launcher.

The squad blew apart, or was thrown off the building, when two dragons swept down to the rooftop, providing added firepower. One rider on a breakerdrake landed beside her. "Angel Wing, right? Do we need to retreat?"

"No, we need support. The original intelligence was only partly right. But we found the central power supply. We need a little more time and a few less drones, though."

The rider nodded, tapping on his dragon's shoulder. Five more dragons split off from the fight, as others tried to pick off drones for them. Kirsty gestured toward the stadium, and guided Deathwhistle down into the nearest alleyway, hoping the cover would last while she did her best to see to her poor firedrake's numerous injuries. "Help is on the way guys," she whispered. "Just hold on."

Charlene rose along the stadium mecha's back as it started to turn. A shot grazed her side, and another hit her hip. DJ took a burn from a near-miss of his own. With no nearby fires to baffle their sensors, two groups of drones had locked in enough to try to corner him, attempting to stop him from being able to circle and dodge around the giant. They closed in as he climbed.

DJ whistled, mimicking the classic bomb-falling sound. Charlene closed her wings and started to plummet. The drones tried to make a quick adjustment to follow or to pull away. Two weren't fast enough and crashed into one another mid-air.

DJ threw up an arm to shield himself from shrapnel, one piece of burning metal tearing into his forearm, as Charlene flared her wings, sweeping along the ground. She was almost thrown out of the air as the mecha turned and fired, hitting the ground where she'd just been. The breakerdrake recovered and started rising again. A few more shots blazed past the dragon and rider as they flew.

Seeing a trio of drones gaining altitude faster still, then turning to dive, firing all the way, DJ got an idea.

"Play chicken, Char," he said, pulling himself to hunch over the saddle. The dragon weaved side to side, evading the shots and heading at the drones. Charlene managed to shoot one down and kept rising to them. DJ glanced back, seeing the mecha raising its arm and homing in on him.

"Fetch, fetch!" he shouted. The dragon screeched as close-up fire from the drones struck, but she managed to stay airborne, dodging out of the flight path and grabbing hold of the lead drone. Instead of tearing it apart, DJ guided Charlene into a dive, powerful wings fighting against the drone's efforts to turn. The other drone shifted position, trying to target them. DJ leaned, and the dragon responded, turning the drone as the mecha fired. The skin on DJ's arm reddened and blistered from the close call, but the shot took out the pursuing drone. Charlene's sustained shriek told him she'd been hurt too, but she was still flying, and her wings were whole.

"A little longer, girl. Let's ride this one home."

Charlene struggled to keep the drone on a collision course, despite the best efforts of its engines. When the crash was inevitable, he finally let Charlene break away—and she tore off a section of the drone's wing, just to be sure. The drone was left to crash into the mecha's head. Charlene shielded him from the heat and shrapnel of the explosion. As they lifted away from the mecha, he could see the effects. The drone had fused with the giant head, denting and twisting in a portion of the armor from the high speed collision, and the drone body was still burning.

The mecha staggered, then collapsed backward, falling against the grandstand walls. To his regret, it started to rise again, though clumsily.

More drones came at them without the obstacle. DJ felt the heat of shots whizzing past and a couple of impacts against the saddle. Charlene's flight grew less steady, dipping to one side as they dove for the cover of the grandstand.

Mari's cover wasn't going to last. The first shot from one of the heavy droids blew out a section of the cement column in front of her, peppering dragon and rider with tiny fragments of rock. Talaitha's return blasts destroyed one of the hunters, but showed no signs of being able to even damage the heavier robots, which advanced steadily.

There was a monstrous crash from above, and the stone began to crack.

"Talaitha, stay close," Mari muttered as she hugged the remnants of the pillar. A portion of the ceiling collapsed, dropping tons of rock on top of some hunters and one of the heavy guardians. She briefly thought there might be more—but the stone settled again, leaving them still outnumbered and outgunned, if not quite as badly.

She pointed out the hunters to Talaitha and pleaded in Romany, "Keep them off me."

Mari climbed over the rubble, rushing right at the big robot. She dove and rolled as it fired, blowing up a section of fallen stone where she'd been and sending more shrapnel flying. A brief glance at the door told her everything she needed to know. Even if they lucked out and won the fight, Talaitha wouldn't be able to cut through the reinforced security door.

She darted away from shattered hiding spots, trying to stay on her feet over the shifting rubble. She slipped and fell, hitting the pile of stones hard, as the robot lined up a shot. The shot went wide when Talaitha crashed into its side, abandoning the other fight long enough to rescue her rider. Mari got to her feet and dove, barely avoiding another blast. Talaitha took more injuries in shielding her rider from the hunters as Mari firmly attached the second-to-last of her bombs, set on its shortest timer, to the guardian's back, then grabbed onto the dragon's saddle. She couldn't pull herself up fast enough, so she just urged Talaitha to run as the blast went off behind her.

Talaitha turned to protect Mari from the blast and ended up rolling along the hallway, wings pulled in, with Mari tucked firmly to the dragon's side. When they came to a stop, the dragon struggled to get to her feet. Mari couldn't tell where any robot reinforcements were, unable to hear after the proximity to the blast. She was just sure they were coming.

She patted Talaitha's head, urging her to watch the stairs as Mari stumbled in as close an approximation as she could make to running. Finding the remnants of the guardian, more intact than she'd have thought, Mari assessed the door again. She had to put all her strength behind moving the robot's arm and heavy weapon to point toward the doors. Pushing the hand against the trigger pad was easier, and the first shot caused the doors to partially buckle. A second shot blew one door off its hinges. Mari raced into the room, finding the main generator, drawing the last and largest of the bombs out of her pack. She set the timer, trying to allow time to get out of the blast radius, while not leaving enough time for hunters to get to it, and raced out of the room toward her dragon.

Talaitha was back on her feet and looking steadier. Two hunters lay at the base of the stairs in ruins, and looking upward, Mari could see shadows moving, as more of them approached. Pulling herself into the saddle, and sure her dragon was as temporarily deaf as she was, she signaled with her feet to charge.

Charlene hit the ground hard, wing joint finally giving out after the shoulder injuries. The hard fall knocked the wind out of DJ, and when the breakerdrake fell, he was pretty sure the landing had broken the leg trapped under her as well. Charlene was trying to right herself, but it wasn't quick, and more drones were closing on them.

Explosions lit the sky as two uneven formations of dragons swept in, ambushing the drones. With some cover, he finally looked to where Ada had fallen, gratified to see the dragon dragging herself toward them, with Rachel showing signs of stirring in the saddle.

The mecha rose from the stadium where it had fallen, a hand coming up, peeling the flaming drone away and tossing it to the side. A sensor light flickered, then regained full strength like a single evil eye, and the giant raised its arm, pointing toward the incoming dragons.

The grandstand shook, and the giant went still, arm still outstretched. Drones started crashing to earth all around them, skidding to a halt. Another explosion shook the ground, and flames started to rise from the stadium.

Like an ocean suddenly evaporating after they'd

been submerged in it some time, the humming stopped.

Dragon riders jumped off their dragons as the creatures stood watch. The men and women ran over to check DJ, Rachel, and their dragons, finally helping Charlene back to her feet.

"We need to get in there. We're still missing one of our squad," DJ could barely hear himself shouting.

The nearest man shook his head, trying to urge him out of Charlene's saddle. DJ shook his head, and guided his unsteady dragon to the nearest doors. Even wounded, Charlene was more than strong enough to toss rubble aside and tear the heavy metal doors off their hinges.

The light from outside cut into the darkness, and a single form moved toward it. Talaitha pulled herself along the hallway, dragging a limp Mari.

Mari blinked awake, intently aware of a pounding in her head, and a general soreness all over. She also quickly became aware that one leg and one arm were immobilized. After that, she realized there were two people by her bedside.

The names she first called at the fuzzy figures were

old and familiar. She remembered quickly that they were wrong.

"They have candles burning in the vigil," Kirsty said. "All your old squad do. And everyone else lost this week. It's…a very *candleful* vigil. But a hopeful one."

"Speed-drakes have been sent to the five nearest cells, sharing what we learned," DJ said. "With any luck, there'll be more assaults soon."

On mention of speed-drakes, Mari tried to prop herself up more, with limited success. "Talaitha?"

"She's in the healing soup. Five or six days in, she'll be good as new. Lot quicker than any of us," DJ said. Mari couldn't help but notice DJ's crutches and leg cast, and the patches over the burns on his arm, or the heavy bandaging at Kirsty's shoulder to go with the arm sling.

Kirsty smiled. "Don't worry, she's in a vat right next to the rest of the squad. At first, they tried to put her in her original squad room, but she wouldn't relax, and Ada threw a fit until they moved things around."

"The rest of the squad accepting her all right?" Mari asked, still a little worried, but less so, hearing about Ada.

"Deathwhistle will. But she ate three meals, and then fell asleep the second she was in familiar territory, and Charlene isn't saying anything with her mouth full. She won't let go of that scrap of the drone we hit the mecha with, like a puppy with a ball." DJ beamed with pride. "I tried to tell her she didn't take down a mecha all by herself, but damned if she'll believe me. Anyway, pretty normal for Ada to make the official statement for them."

"Speaking of Ada, is Rachel okay?" Mari said.

"She's fine, but they need all the tech people they can get. Rachel is down helping analyze the pieces of the mechas we took apart, trying to find more weaknesses, or break into the AIs' communications net."

"Are they worried Calgary got off a message of exactly what we were doing at the end? That the other cities will reconfigure their power sources before anyone can get there?"

"They're worried about everything. How can they not be? But the point stands that the Calgary AI can't get back up. For the rest, if anyone can figure it out, Rachel will," Kirsty said. "She'll come visit at dinner time."

Mari relaxed again, wincing at a twinge in her leg as she settled. "So I guess the dragons have decided."

"Yep," DJ said. "You're an Angel now."

Lee French slaves away on her laptop from a Beanbag of Comfort +4 in Olympia, WA. She writes fantasy and science fiction with action and snark. Every once in a while, she pretends to be serious, but it never lasts longer than a short story. Find out more about her work at www.authorleefrench.com and follow her on Twitter @AuthorLeeFrench.

Alien Dragons

LEE FRENCH

"I could stay here for about ever." Bobby took a long pull from his beer, reveling in the midday sunshine. His beach chair sat in a clearing to the side of the sprawling farmhouse, where a handful of the other residents at this retreat for superheroes lay on towels or chairs to enjoy the fine, early autumn weather.

Lily, curled up on his lap, clinked her bottle against his. "I like that plan." Her delicate West Coast accent made Bobby's heavy Georgia drawl sound barbaric. She raked her fingernails across his scalp and kissed his cheek.

Beside them, her little boy played with two of Bobby's dragons. Sebastian hopped to his feet and leaned on the arm of Bobby's chair. "Make them go! I want to chase."

Bobby grinned and gave the two dragons, each the size of a quarter, a mental command to run the kid ragged so he'd take a nap later. One tiny silver dart streaked away, glittering in the light. The other hovered in front of Sebastian's face and stuck its silver tongue out at the boy, then flew off at a pace the boy could keep up with. Bobby watched Sebastian shriek with delight and run.

With the toddler safely out of sight, Bobby kissed Lily, savoring the peace and quiet along with the beautiful woman at hand. Only a month ago, he'd told off the President of the United States in the living room of the Chairman of the Joint Chiefs because government agents had spent the previous two months chasing him and several others of the group across the country to use them as lab rats. Among other things. Now the US public knew Bobby Mitchell as the "spokesdragon" for the entire group of over two hundred people with superpowers.

"Security to the front," Sam's voice murmured through the earbud Bobby wore as part of the security team for the grounds. She could monitor umpteen video feeds while making lunch and holding a conversation. "We have incoming guests. One vehicle, looks military."

Bobby broke off the kiss. "Heckbiscuits, they got crappy timing. Don't go nowhere."

"I won't." Lily balanced on the arms of the chair while Bobby let his body fall apart into hundreds of tiny silver dragons. The swarm streamed around the huge farmhouse, through the unpaved parking area, and to the end of the drive connecting their property to the nearby rural highway in the middle of nowhere, northeastern Colorado. At that point, he re-formed the dragons into his body, feet-first.

Stephen dropped out of the sky to land beside him in his black, hooded trenchcoat, though his feet didn't touch the ground. The pasty-white vampire always floated, even when he didn't have to. "Is there anything better than an unannounced, unrequested visit by members of the military?"

"I can think of about fifty things offhand." Down the unpaved, tree-lined drive, Bobby saw a tan Humvee rumbling toward them. He tapped his earbud to allow it to send his voice through vibrations in his jaw bone, or something like that. Greg, their resident brainiac, had made them, and Bobby only understood the important part—how to use it.

"Sam," Bobby said, feeling stupid as always for talking to someone nowhere near him without using a phone. "Stephen and I got eyes on the vehicle. Don't look like they're planning on ramming nothing. Them things is pretty bumpy, so I ain't surprised they're taking it slow." He'd driven a Humvee once and had no desire to repeat the activity.

"On my way," Jayce said in his ear.

To the side, a nine-foot tall monster of muscle,

claws, fangs, and fur stepped out of the trees. The werewolf shrank into Matthew as he walked, the former Marine wearing only his desert fatigue pants and a sheen of sweat from what had to have been a rigorous workout.

"Army," Matthew spat. He crossed his arms over his well-muscled chest and waited in a shaft of sunlight with Bobby and Stephen.

"Show-off," Stephen muttered.

"Bloodsucker," Matthew said.

The Humvee stopped in front of them, cutting off the friendly sniping. Through the front windshield, Bobby saw four people, two in front and two in back. The driver stayed in the vehicle, leaving it running, while the other three stepped out. One man had enough ribbons and rank doodads on his blue jacket to mark him as a high-level officer. The other two wore green jungle fatigues and carried weapons.

"I'm going to stay out of sight for the moment," Jayce reported into Bobby's ear.

"Sounds good," Bobby murmured. He stepped forward and resisted the urge to swagger, adjust his jeans, or puff out his chest. "Can't say we were expecting company," he shouted over the engine noise.

The officer gave Bobby a polite smile and pointed to the farmhouse. "Can we talk inside?"

"No, you sure as heckbiscuits ain't coming inside our house. Either you or this thing is going back down the driveway. Or we can stand here and shout at each other, I suppose."

His smile turning sour, the officer flicked a hand at one of his two escorts. The soldier thumped the Humvee's hood and pointed for it to retreat. Everyone waited while the vehicle backed away slower than it had come. When the noise faded to a light rumble on the wind, the soldier gave a hand signal for it to stop.

"Whoever you are, you better have a darn good reason for being here. Not only are you not supposed to know where this place is, we done told you we'd come to you folks as soon as we're ready to. And you're spoiling what was a pretty good day."

"Major Kenner," the officer said, holding out his hand to shake. All three men ignored it. He withdrew the gesture and tucked his hat under his arm. His back stick-straight, he gave them all a stern looking-over. "I was asked to come here and make you an offer. Are you willing to listen?"

"You got two minutes."

Kenner nodded. "The wormhole technology you're already aware of has been completed. We can hold the rift stable for a short time and we've successfully tested it with small inanimate objects. Due to the…unusual qualities several of your people exhibit, we'd like to extend an invitation to you to send a team through the rift in lieu of soldiers, on the chance the environment on the other side is not as hospitable to normal human life as suspected."

Bobby blinked at him. Not only had he thought those scientists needed more time to perfect the wormhole tech, he'd figured he'd have to find out about it the hard way and clean up after the fact from whatever dumbass things the military, government, or scientists did on the other side. To get an invitation to make that first contact blindsided him.

"Oh. Hum. That's…"

"Surprising," Stephen supplied.

"Violet is coming out," Sam said into his ear. "She said not to agree to anything until she gets there. Stall for a minute."

"Welp, Major Kenner, I guess we got some things to talk about after all." Bobby squinted at him, wondering what brought the man directly to their front door. The military shouldn't have eyes on their compound from satellites, since Sam said she'd hacked into a bunch of places to make sure this whole area got skipped over. They had secure, anonymized internet access and their phones didn't throw a GPS signal. Everything that had to be registered or licensed with any sort of government went through a shell company operating under a nonprofit with some other legal mumbo-jumbo in the way of connecting them to it.

"First things first, though. How'd you find us?"

Kenner shrugged. "I wasn't given that

information."

"What, they just handed you an address?"

"Yes."

"Oh, that doesn't sound suspicious at all," Sam said into his ear.

Bobby scowled. "Fine. Never mind on that. When you go back to your boss, though, you make sure he understands we done kept this place off the grid for a reason, and it ain't only about you folks. Lots of nutty people out there with nutty ideas."

Kenner nodded. "Does this mean you're rejecting the offer?"

Behind him, Bobby heard the screen door bang shut. "No, sir, it surely don't. This is Violet." He jerked a thumb over his shoulder without looking. "She's our chief negotiator. Now we know the broad strokes, she'll want to chat about the finer points."

Kenner's mouth twitched, making him look even less friendly. "What kind of negotiations?"

Violet, a shapely blond woman halfway through a law degree, reached the group and offered her hand to shake with Kenner. As he accepted it, she smiled. "Pleased to meet you, Major Kenner." Her Alabama twang made her sound harmless, as usual. "It's real nice of you to come all this way just to ask us for help. We'd like to give you that help you want, but I'm sure you can understand we can't just hare off and do something for nothing. The world just doesn't work that way."

"Of course. What sort of payment are you looking for?"

"Are you authorized to negotiate compensation for us?"

"Yes, ma'am."

Violet offered him a dazzling smile and looped her arm through his. She tugged him along on a stroll away from his escorts. Bobby, Stephen and Matthew got in the other two soldiers' way, preventing them from following. So he could hear what went on, Bobby let a dragon pop off his finger and sent it to Violet's shoulder. He threw his mind into that dragon, leaving his body to stand there and look implacable.

"Thing is, Major Kenner, we don't need money. We don't want military equipment. We would rather the military stay as far away from us as possible. In fact, we'd mostly just like to be left alone. What we want in exchange for helping out the US government is extraterritoriality."

Kenner stopped and blinked rapidly. "I beg your pardon?"

"All of us are happy to remain taxpaying citizens, we just want the freedom to govern ourselves. With our unusual abilities, most of the rules for normal people just don't cut the mustard, Major Kenner. We need to be able to self-police and handle our problems ourselves without governmental or police intrusion."

"I...wasn't given instruction on this type of compensation." Kenner rubbed his jaw. "I think what you're asking for is to become a new reservation, like Native Americans have. I'm not sure what that would take, but it probably involves negotiating with the Colorado state government. For the moment, I can offer the establishment of a no-fly zone over your compound—"

"Bless your heart," Violet said with a sigh. "We don't want you monitoring our land or skies. We especially don't want you putting up any kind of barriers, even invisible ones. So you run on back to your bosses and you tell them we're coming down to White Sands. Whether we help or hinder there is up to them. Here's a phone number they can call anytime." She handed him a slip of paper. "If they ever send a messenger here unannounced again, we won't be kind. They've got, oh, let's call it six hours to get back to me for honest negotiations. Our boys'll be down there by then, waiting to hear if they ought to be friendly or not."

"Miss—"

"Call me Violet, honey."

"Violet. The US government doesn't respond well to threats."

Violet smiled, sweet as peach pie. "Sugar, whether you realize it or not, you coming here is a threat delivered to us. We don't respond well to that either."

"It doesn't matter who threw the first punch,

Violet." Kenner stiffened and straightened, and he replaced his hat on his head. "It matters who throws the last. I'll deliver your message, but don't believe for one moment we can't find a way to deal with you and your people here. *Humans* have always been good at adapting."

Bobby snapped his mind back to his body with a frown and watched Kenner stride away from Violet. The Major ignored him as he returned to the Humvee with his soldiers. Trying not to let this cast a pall over the mission, Bobby turned away to go pack. He hoped they took the deal.

"I'm sorry about this." Bobby stuffed an extra set of clothes into his backpack. He looked around the bedroom he shared with Lily and Sebastian, trying to imagine what he might need besides clothes.

"It's okay," Lily said, sitting on the bed and holding her son's favorite teddy bear. "Sebastian will be crushed if you don't make it back in time for his birthday, but we'll survive somehow."

"I'll try hard as I can. If'n we're just gonna blow stuff up, I don't imagine it'll be an issue, but I got a feeling they'll at least make enough of an effort for us to cooperate. Tell the truth, I'm kinda nervous about that. Seeing the place we all half came from is kinda…" He packed a few tools he'd picked up in Afghanistan and cinched the bag shut. Nothing came to mind to finish the sentiment.

"I'd like to see that someday." Lily stood and kissed him, her body warm and soft against his. "I know you won't get seriously hurt. Just come back. No matter how invulnerable you think you are, you can still die."

"I know. I seen that up close and personal." He held her close and promised himself he'd remember this moment, no matter what happened. "We'll all look out for each other. S'what we do."

She walked with him to the kitchen, where he grabbed a sandwich from the usual ready-made stack and stuffed it into his mouth. Without being asked and without him thinking to do it himself, Lily snagged two more sandwiches and slid them into a plastic bag for him.

"For when you get there," she said as she tucked the bag into his pack.

Bobby kissed her cheek. "I'd probably leave my head behind if'n you weren't around to keep it attached."

"Don't you forget it."

They wove through the huge farmhouse to the front door, where they found Stephen, Matthew, and Jayce already waiting. Jayce, the lone Native American among the original batch of superpowered people, crouched beside Sebastian, giving the boy a high-five.

"Bobby! Jayce says you're going to get me a special birthday present!" Sebastian ran and jumped with blind trust that Bobby would catch him.

"I sure am." Bobby scooped the boy up. "I don't know if'n we'll get back in time, but I'll try like heckbiscuits. If not, you make sure you get a proper cake. Don't you let nobody convince you it's fine to have whole-grain, free range cupcakes made with kale or nothing. Regular cake."

"Yeah!" The boy hugged Bobby around the neck. "No kale!"

"Be good for your momma or we're gonna have words." Bobby squeezed the boy, kissed his forehead, and handed him off to Lily. They traded waves as he walked away. Though he had every intention of flying down as the swarm, he had to ask Jayce, "How in heckbiscuits did you think of that?"

Jayce shrugged. "That's what my dad always said when his business trips conflicted with family stuff. He'd bring back cheesy tourist crap, but it was special because he said it would be."

"I don't reckon we'll find anything like that where we're going."

"Maybe we can bring him back a piece of the machine if we have to smash it," Stephen said. He wore his

Army desert camouflage, including the full head covering, gloves, and tinted goggles to protect his entire body from the sun. They couldn't see his expression, but Bobby heard his grin, loud and clear.

"Sure." Bobby smirked and handed the vampire his pack. Though his clothes stayed when he went into the swarm, including anything in his pockets, he'd never had a pack come with him. "Let's go straight there, no detours. I'll carry Jayce, you take Matthew."

"Can we call it wolfyback instead of piggyback?" Matthew now wore his full Marines desert camouflage.

"Man, you can call it anything you want. Ain't right to judge." To save himself from Matthew's reaction, he flowed into the swarm and swirled around Jayce.

Jayce's flesh shimmered until it matched his blue windbreaker. His entire body took on the properties of ripstop nylon. Before he could blow away, the dragons snared him and darted upward. Stephen joined them with Matthew on his back. They turned south and sped away.

Their path kept them away from Denver, Colorado Springs, and Pueblo, but they didn't bother avoiding smaller towns. At two-thousand feet up, no one in Trinidad would notice them. As they streaked past Santa Fe, Stephen's phone rang. Their signals bounced off satellites, giving them reception anywhere in the world.

Stephen let the call go to voicemail. When they landed at White Sands Missile Range in twilight, he retrieved his phone and checked the message.

"Violet says we're not getting what we want, but we're getting the best they can grant on short notice. She and our *best friend*, General Hanstadt, are going to work together to get something attached to the next federal budget as an amendment no one will bother reading or voting against. In the meantime, everybody's going to be polite and friendly."

Somehow, Bobby doubted the Chairman of the Joint Chiefs would put his full effort behind their requests, especially given how the meeting with Kenner went. But he still wanted to go through the wormhole. They could give the man the benefit of the doubt.

Jayce returned to flesh next to Bobby and shrugged. "Sounds like the best we're going to get anytime soon."

"I guess we ain't here to cause a ruckus then. Maybe we ought to introduce ourselves to the locals and get us an escort." Bobby led the group to the nearest building. Within fifteen minutes, a jeep arrived with a starstruck Private Somers who knew Bobby from seeing him on TV. They piled in and let the soldier take a selfie with them. Bobby ate his sandwiches during the ride.

The curvy road to the bunker hadn't changed since the last time Bobby was here. He hoped to have a chance to see Mike, a data analyst working here who had some kind of weird online computer nerd relationship with

Sam. The guy should have alerted them to the successful tests, but Sam hadn't said anything about him being in trouble.

Private Somers drove them to the front door of a concrete building and a guard opened the door for them. Even though this type of welcome had been promised, Bobby couldn't help but check behind doors, watching for men in suits to jump out and stab him with a needle full of drugs. He'd been taught to expect a trap and it bothered him not to find one.

"Hi!" The man in the lab coat who rushed into the hall to greet them crashed into the wall in his haste. He bounced off and straightened his dark hair and glasses while clearing his throat. "I mean hello. I'm Dr. Eisenberg." The spindly man offered his hand to shake.

After looking the man over and checking for hidden syringes, Bobby shook his hand. "Nice to meet you, doctor."

"Excuse me for being so excited," Eisenberg gushed. "The wormhole is working, I've never met a half-alien before, and I can hardly wait to see what you bring back. There's so much opportunity here! A whole new world, new plants, new animals, new everything. And we don't even need spaceships. My friends at NASA will be so jealous."

He shook hands with Stephen, Matthew, and Jayce while continuing to prattle. "I'm absolutely fascinated by how your mutations were triggered, and how it's even possible for a mutation to change a person's digestive system so completely that you can only handle blood. I'm no biologist, but it's still amazing."

"Doc, we're real happy to be participating in this, but excuse us for not being wild about indulging scientists and curiosity and all that about our powers. We been poked and prodded enough, thanks. How about you tell us what's what with the wormhole?"

"Actually, if you happen to have a pretty lab assistant handy, I'd be glad to demonstrate how it works." Stephen had pulled his balaclava down and perched his goggles on his forehead. He gave Eisenberg a dark grin. "I'm a little hungry."

Matthew rolled his eyes. "Don't listen to him. He just fed yesterday." He gave Stephen a stern look. "From his girlfriend."

"What? Kris understands."

"Gentlemen." Jayce put one hand on each man's shoulder from behind. "Later. Right now, Dr. Eisenberg is going to explain what we're about to do. It might be important to listen."

"Ah, yes." Eisenberg coughed and blushed. "This way." He led them to a large room filled with electronic equipment. At the center of the massive tangle of mismatched pipes, cables, metal sheeting, and robotic arms, three concentric rings of metal stood on a pillar.

They appeared to be anchored to each other to they'd all spin in different directions without crashing. Bobby had seen something like it in a movie once. Parts of the whole apparatus seemed more advanced than others, as if some pieces had been assembled fifty years ago, and others as recently as last week. Considering this program had been in process since Roswell, that could be the case.

Six other people in lab coats with clipboards and tablets stopped everything they were doing to watch the spectacle of four half-aliens with superpowers enter the room.

Eisenberg pointed to the three-ring structure. "In simple laymen's terms, that part will generate the wormhole. So far, we've sent a rock and an unopened can of beer. Nothing bad happened, and we were able to determine the air is within the range for human breathability. So, we're ready to try a robot, but even though the Mars Rover has been a success, we don't keep those lying around and NASA won't give us one. You all were the next best option."

"Whoa." Bobby frowned. "When we were asked to come here, it sounded like you'd sent some things through and got them back. This sounds more like you sent some things through and nothing done blew up."

"Yes," Eisenberg bobbed his head enthusiastically. "We sent two things through and nothing blew up. Without a means of locomotion on the other end, we can't get them back. That's where you come in. We can open the wormhole for thirty-seven point six seconds. Once it closes, we have to realign six parts, replace two others, and recharge the battery so we don't wipe out power for the entire base, Alamogordo, Las Cruces, Albuquerque, and a handful of small towns. This process takes about three days."

"Thirty-some seconds don't sound like long enough to do nothing but all of us go through."

"That's the idea. You all go through, it shuts down, you take readings and record video for us, then three days later, we open it up and you come back. If we miss you that time, we can try again three days later."

"We're going to need supplies." Matthew set his pack down. "There may not be any potable water or edible food near the site. If we'd known this was the situation, we would've packed for it. We all thought it would be a one-day thing."

"If you make a list of supplies, it can all be gathered for you. Let's plan to open the wormhole tomorrow morning at seven. Some of our extremely efficient military gentlemen will get whatever you need. If you follow me, I'll show you a place you can get some sleep."

"Excuse me." Stephen sidled up to the lone woman in the room. He tapped her shoulder, then took her hand and kissed it. "Can I possibly interest you in sacrificing your evening for the greater good?"

Bobby snapped on a tactical vest with bulging pockets and covered it with an Army jacket. The matching pants had pockets full of food, water, and tools. Stephen and Jayce, both of whom could handle the extra weight without issue, hefted packs filled with additional gear. Matthew got the same type of vest as Bobby, as well as weapons he shared with Jayce. Bobby and Stephen had neither the training nor the need to carry guns.

The female lab assistant gave Stephen a sultry smile, promising without words that he could tap her veins anytime. Eisenberg ordered the countdown to begin from twenty. Jayce fidgeted with the camera clipped to his coat. Bobby took a deep breath and tried not to think about how he'd be jumping into a hole made by something that ought to smash him into pieces to travel bajillions of miles across space in a few seconds to the planet his mother came from.

Electronic things whirred. Green and amber lights winked on. Metal pistons popped and ka-chunked. At the count of fifteen, the inner circle made a lazy revolution. It sped until the count of ten, when the middle circle started.

The outer circle made its first turn at five. When Eisenberg reached zero, the three rings rotated so fast Bobby couldn't see the inner one.

Blue light rippled in the center, darker tendrils writhing around the edges. The middle ring disappeared. As the outer ring disappeared, the blue became a disc with white mist in the center.

"Go, go, go!" Eisenberg shouted.

Bobby shook his wonder and jumped through. After a moment of gut-roiling vertigo, he landed in a circle of churned earth surrounded by trees in dappled sunshine and one can of beer lying on its side. Stephen hit him from behind, knocking him to the ground. When Matthew fell through, the impact forced a grunt out of Bobby. He wriggled to get free. Jayce landed on the pile with a groan. Bobby looked back in time to see an orange-rimmed disc showing the lab and Dr. Eisenberg moments before it disappeared with an audible pop.

In the now-empty space, he saw instead a smooth, silver tree among the more normal-looking ones. This silver trunk ended in four thick roots, three pointing in one direction and the fourth opposite. As he craned his neck up, he thought the knobby section about fifteen feet up seemed like a backward-bending knee. Then he kept following it and realized that silver thing wasn't a tree. It was a leg. Those roots were claws.

He gulped. "Uh, guys?" he whispered.

The body attached to the leg had huge, powerful muscles, and the overall shape of what he could see reminded him of a giant dinosaur. If the wormhole things had been naturally occurring on some long-term schedule, maybe whatever-sauruses had wandered here from Earth at some point, accidentally preserving their species.

Matthew shoved Jayce, getting the bigger man to move. Stephen stared up in awe. "I always knew we needed a Godzilla. Werewolves and vampires are so last decade."

"It might not be friendly," Jayce warned.

"Animals care about whether something is predator or prey," Stephen said. "Friendly isn't really an issue. If it eats plants, we're safe so long as we don't startle it. If it eats meat, we'll have to deal with it."

As Stephen spoke, the creature shifted. Bobby watched a long, narrow head poke through the trees, big enough to snap up at least two of them in one bite. For a moment, the head reminded him of an alligator, then he recognized the frill of horns pointing back from its head and the pure silver of its eyes and nostrils.

"It's a dragon," he murmured. "Just like mine."

"Can you talk to it?" Jayce asked.

"How? It's fifty thousand times bigger'n mine."

"That's kind of an exaggeration," Stephen said as he floated slowly away from the giant dragon.

"Ain't the time," Bobby snapped.

Jayce's flesh shimmered to steel. Matthew inched toward a tree to hide behind. The dragon's mouth opened, revealing more silver inside, just like Bobby's dragons. Six-inch, jagged teeth lined its jaws. If this thing was a really big version of Bobby's dragons, it used them to grind metal.

The stench of rotting eggs filled the air, then the world exploded in fire. Bobby flew apart into tiny dragons —immune to fire—and sent the swarm up. They split into two halves to cluster around the big dragon's eyes and confuse it. The dragon jerked its head back and snapped at the swarm, crushing a handful and swallowing them.

Tiny dragon trills of righteous fury filled the air. They flew at its eyes, scraping claws too small to cause harm across the surface. The big dragon squeezed its eyes shut, crushing half a dozen dragons with each lid. Then it shook its head and caught several in its mouth.

Stephen jumped on the dragon's back and tried to bite its neck, but he pulled away, holding his mouth. On the ground, the werewolf scraped his claws and fangs against the metal of its leg to no avail. Jayce fired two rounds from his pistol, both of which ricocheted off its hide without causing any harm.

"Run!" Jayce shouted.

Bobby sent what was left of the swarm after Jayce. Matthew and Stephen caught up. They sprinted through the woods. Behind them, the dragon's feet thumped on the ground. Trees cracked and groaned with its passage.

"What the hell!" Stephen shouted. "It's invulnerable?"

"No idea," Jayce managed as he pumped his arms and legs. "Distract if it gets closer."

"That's easy for you to say," Stephen snapped. "Do you have any idea what fire does to vampires?"

"Not real ones."

"Me neither. I don't want to find out!"

Unable to communicate like this, Bobby ignored them. As soon as they reached some kind of safety, they'd regroup and figure out what to do. He had no intention of missing the next wormhole home.

The dragon still lumbered behind them, though it slowed as if it lost interest when it couldn't see them. Then Bobby's swarm slammed into a wall he never saw coming. The others kept going, running right through whatever the swarm had hit. Stunned by the impact, the tiny dragons fell to the ground and wobbled like drunken sailors.

He re-formed his body and sat up, crawling on his hands and knees to find the barrier. Nothing stood in his way anymore. Immediately to his left, the dragon's head bounced off the nothing just as Bobby's swarm had and it roared in frustration. Bobby scrambled forward. If this barrier stopped dragons and nothing else, he wanted to be on the other side of it.

When the dragon turned and loped away, Bobby breathed a sigh of relief. He toppled over and lay in the grass, feeling the aches in his hands and arms flow in as his adrenaline ebbed. Too many dragons had been lost in that fight, and for nothing. They hadn't even scratched that thing.

"Man, did anyone catch the plate for that dragon?"

Stephen dropped to a crouch beside him. "Are you okay?"

"It smashed a good number of my dragons. My hands hurt like heckbiscuits."

Jayce and Matthew returned to his side. "Why did you stop?" Matthew asked.

"There's some sorta something that my dragons hit. That dragon hit it too. I guess we got a lot in common. I got no idea what we hit, though."

"Good thing we didn't bring any science types." Jayce approached a tree and ran his hands over the trunk. Wisps of his long, black hair, loose from the tail tied at the nape of his neck, rose and danced in the air. "There's some kind of electrical or magnetic field here. I can feel the vibration. It's in the tree? I don't know how that works. Greg would probably be able to explain this."

Matthew moved from tree to tree, scanning the area without straying out of sight. "Guys, if someone set up a field that repels dragons, it's reasonable to assume they're inside that field. If we guess it's a circular field, either emanating from a central point or not, the angle of this arc suggests it's a pretty big area. I don't see a path, though."

"If that's true, we should find the owners if we go that way," Stephen said, pointing away from the dragon barrier.

"It could be any type of sentient beings." Jayce offered Bobby a hand up. "Are you good to keep going, or do we need to take a breather?"

Bobby gripped Jayce's hand and winced as he took the help to get to his feet. He looked around, finally able to take a minute to check out their surroundings. Errant rays of sunshine pierced the canopy, throwing a gentle glow over the bright green flora. The temperature felt just right, like a perfect spring day. Crickets buzzed a dozen yards away and the rich aroma of damp earth mingled with a woody pine scent.

"You know, these trees look mostly like normal trees, except the leaves ain't quite right. And those flowers? I ain't no expert, but I never seen nothing like that before."

He paced to a stand of yellow flowers, each with four ruffled, curled petals shaped to collect rain and funnel it down the stalk. When he prodded one, the petals wrapped around his finger and a burst of copper hit the air. Tiny pinpricks surprised him, but didn't cause enough harm to force his dragons out. In fact, aside from the initial shock of such strange plant behavior, it felt pleasant. As warmth suffused his finger, the petals turned white and shriveled.

Pulling his finger away, he watched the dried white petals drift to the ground. "I *know* I ain't never seen a plant do *that*." He stooped to pick up a petal and noticed the ache had drained from his hand. With his fingers splayed, he turned his hand over and furrowed his brow.

"This plant works kinda like Liam's power. He takes an injury on himself and regenerates it. This plant seems to take an injury on itself and dump the flower, maybe to make a new one."

Stephen floated beside him. "In a certain sort of way, it makes sense we'd find plants and animals here that echo our powers. After all, they had to come from somewhere. I don't understand how this makes complete sense, but I only know basic science. It's possible the plant left a marker in your DNA or something, I suppose. That doesn't explain the dragon and you, but I doubt there's anything that could." He flashed fang in a grin.

"Whatever." Bobby rolled his eyes. "We should try to find the elves. I bet they can steer us clear of this world's vampires, werewolves, and whatever else is awful."

"The thing that makes ice would be interesting."

"Unless it's a yeti what can make blizzards."

"Fair point. An ice cube creating yak, on the other hand, has a lot of entertainment potential."

"The grass is normal enough," Matthew said. "We should walk on it. That way. If you two are done playing with the flowers, that is."

"Hey, it ain't my fault you don't got a girlfriend."

Matthew clenched his jaw and stalked away.

Jayce raised an eyebrow.

"Smooth, Bobby," Stephen murmured. "Real smooth. Like glass."

Bobby smacked himself in the forehead. He knew Matthew's fiancee had been murdered about six months ago. Hurrying to catch up, he called ahead, "Man, I'm sorry. I didn't mean that." He froze when he saw that Matthew stood with his hands up, the business end of the weirdest shotgun he'd ever seen pointed at the Marine's face. The elf holding it flicked his gaze over Bobby and scowled.

"You're trespassing, humans," the elf said. In English, with a light Tex-Mex accent.

Bobby let his mouth fall open. "What?"

"Trespassing." The elf raised his brow and made a face like he thought Bobby might be stupid. "Moving through lands where you don't have permission to be."

"We know what trespassing means," Stephen said, holding his hands up in surrender. "We just didn't expect you to."

"How in heckbiscuits do you speak English?"

The elf stared at them. He wore leathers styled like

a Wild West cowboy and dyed to match the greens and browns of the forest. The points of his ears stuck out over his short blonde hair. His shotgun had a single barrel with a flared end made of green-tinted metal. Opaque green tubes, smooth and as thick as Bobby's finger, snaked around the barrel from the stock. That stock appeared to be made of tree bark.

"Who are you people and what are you doing here?"

"I'm Bobby. This is Matthew, Stephen, and Jayce. We're from Earth. Our smart folks figured out a way to open a portal between our two worlds on purpose. They done sent us through to see what's here and all that."

"You should go back. Tell your 'smart folks' there are too many hostile creatures here and it's not worth the effort."

Bobby raised his hands. "I don't rightly think that's gonna work. They got some powerful weapons, and if they think everything here is hostile, they're gonna send people through to cause a right ruckus and wipe you folks out. Since we're kin of a sort, you and us, we'd like that not to happen."

The elf's eyes flicked up and down Matthew. "What do you mean by kin? I see you have eyes like ours when Ernie didn't, but everything else about you seems human."

"Would it be asking too much for you to lower the

gun?" Matthew asked. "We're not here to harm anyone. We came to talk."

"You have guns. People don't bring guns to talk."

Furrowing his brow, Bobby tried to understand the situation. Some human named Ernie had been here, somehow. This guy gave them an awful lot of information, it sounded like. "Can we talk to Ernie? He might understand the things we come here to say better."

"No. He died several years ago. You can talk to me. If I decide you should, you can talk to our Elders."

Bobby lowered his hands and tucked his thumbs into his back pockets. "Okay. How's this? All of us were born from one of your people, name of Asyllis. Her mate, Tarilyr, died on our world and she was forced to breed with humans, which is where we came from." That didn't cover the entire picture, but he didn't want to confuse the guy too much.

The elf blinked and rested his gun against his shoulder. "Asyllis and Tarilyr are my parents." His face twisted into a mask of rage. "She was 'forced' to bear children? What animal did this?"

"People who are already dead," Jayce said. "There's no one to have revenge on. We're sorry to bring you this awful news. Your mother died recently, but your father has been dead for a long time. Since shortly after he disappeared."

"If'n you'll let us, we'd like to get to know you,

since we're half-brothers."

The elf hung his head. "When they disappeared, we all feared the worst. Fate gave us Ernie in exchange, which wasn't so bad. I would've preferred my parents, though. And I always held out hope."

"When they went missing, you got Ernie?" Bobby guessed the original wormhole must have pulled some dumbass from Roswell here when it pulled Asyllis and Tarilyr there. "I guess that explains a lot. I don't suppose you know his last name? We can let his family know what happened to him, just like you're finding out about yours."

"You should see the Elders. This way." The elf turned and stormed away.

"Ain't that a pair of buttered britches."

"What?" Matthew asked. Stephen and Jayce both looked at him, then shrugged and followed the elf.

Bobby also shrugged. "Who'd'a figured the first elf we meet happens to be the son Asyllis told me about before she died? That's almost as crazy as them speaking English."

Matthew shook his head and fell into step behind Jayce. Bobby walked alongside him, trying not to trample too much or make a lot of noise. Past a clump of shrubs, they found a flagstone path running to the right and left. Tidy, unbroken hedges reaching ten feet tall and covered with tiny white blossoms blocked passage straight ahead. Bobby resisted the urge to send up a dragon to scout, thinking elves living behind a barrier to prevent dragon intrusion might not like that so much.

Above the hedge, he noticed a tree trunk so big around it took them twenty paces to pass it. He gawked, never having seen anything that big before. The tree stretched so high he had no idea how tall it was. At least forty feet up, the lowest branch had so much girth it could've held that giant dragon without issue. He pictured his momma's house sitting up there and figured he wouldn't even be able to see it from below.

Bobby walked into Stephen when the vampire slowed to go through a gap in the hedge. The path leading through and away from the hedge appeared to be made of a green-tinted metal, but when Bobby stepped on it, the surface turned out to be spongy. He didn't waste his time trying to guess what it might be—he had plenty of other things to stare at.

High in the giant trees, bridges ran from one huge branch to another, all shimmering like the material from the walkway. Thick green vines clung to the undersides. Metal cables lifted a brown bark cupola big enough to hold six people, carrying it from the forest floor to the base of a branch. In the distance, Bobby heard engines purring and metal clacking together.

Rounded huts made of hundreds of trained vines and covered with flowers clustered around the bases of the trees. Surrounding them, gardens held plants in every shade of green with flowers in every other color. Bobby noticed several frosted glass globes perched on short, woody plants in neat rows along flagstone paths to the huts and had no idea what to make of it.

Elven children ran past, shrieking with joy. Other elves worked in gardens. Many paused to watch the group parade by with curiosity. Bobby could imagine all the horrible things the military might do here, and the worse things regular humans might do out of fear or hate for anybody different. He grew up around people who hated folks for the color of their skin. Elves might be treated even worse than that for having pointy ears.

They reached a shallow pit flanked by cables as the cupola returned to the ground. Their guide peeled away the basket's door, which seemed to be a flap of bark with a hook to hold it in place. Inside, smooth wood formed benches. Bobby sat and leaned over the edge to watch. Stephen stood in the center while Matthew and Jayce sat.

As soon as their guide hooked the bark door in place, the cupola shuddered and rose, suspended between the cables. Bobby had seen plenty of awe-inspiring vistas from higher than this, but he still drank in the sight. The town snaked around the giant trees with graceful curves and spots of color among more shades of green than he expected. From above, it reminded him of abstract paintings he'd never understood yet always found pleasant to stare at. He wanted to share this with Lily.

The giant branch introduced them to another different world. Dark vines wrapped around steel beams and more frosted globes perched on bark-encrusted stands. At the tree's trunk, the wood bulged out with a door suggesting a room inside and a set of steps winding around the trunk to a higher branch. Along the branch they now stood on, giant leaves clustered to form ten to fifteen foot high mounds that could be structures. Anywhere without leaf mounds had a steel railing wrapped with flowering vines.

Following their guide, the foursome walked up the steps, passing the next higher branch in favor of the smaller one above it. Instead of a long walkway surrounded by leaf mounds, this branch had only one structure. Giant leaves covered a lattice of vines to form a large shelter.

Three elves sat in ornate, cushioned wood chairs on the trunk side of the shelter. Two other chairs stood empty. These three elves wore fine cloth in bright blue and green. Lines creased their faces and their white hair hung long and limp. The one man's hand trembled. The two women's shoulders hunched.

Their guide led them across the shelter and rose a hand to stop them several feet from the three older elves. He spoke in a melodious language full of light, lilting sounds.

The woman sitting in the center peered with filmy

eyes as she responded. Bobby clasped his hands behind his back, trying to wait patiently while the elves chatted. Their guide clearly had a great deal of respect for these elders. Without knowing what questions they asked, Bobby couldn't tell if they deserved any from him.

"Halfbreeds," the woman in the middle said, using the word as if it were a form of address for something lower than herself.

"I'm partial to being called Bobby." He gave the names for the other three, hoping someone might reciprocate this time.

All the elves stared at him in silence for a long time. "What do you want here?" the center woman finally asked.

"We're explorers, ma'am. Just looking to get the lay of the land and figure out what's what here. If'n you could tell us about the dragon what chased us into your town, we'd appreciate that."

Again, a thick silence settled over them. After another few minutes, the elves chatted with each other. Their guide ended the conversation with a bow from his waist and shooed the group out. He said nothing as they climbed into the cupola again, and continued not to speak as they reached the ground and walked back the way they'd come.

At the tall hedge and flagstone path, he pointed. "You're to leave and not return. The Elders have spoken."

"Whoa. Wait a minute." Bobby crossed his arms. "You don't want to do that. You kick us out and our bosses'll come back with machine guns and bombs. They ain't real understanding. They'll blow everything up. We want to be friends, not enemies."

"The Elders find it inexcusable that two of our people were killed on your world and my mother was forced to mate with your people. And I agree." The elf pointed away from the town. "Leave."

Jayce held up a hand. "Is there anything we could possibly do to show our intention to become your allies? We had nothing to do with these events. Your father died before any of us was born. Your mother's death was accidental. And our only involvement with the other matter is being the product of it."

The elf scowled and crossed his arms. He tapped his foot.

"We ain't leaving until you give us some sorta something to go on."

"The dragon," the elf said after a long pause. "If you could somehow slay or tame the dragon so we no longer need the barrier, that would prove your intentions are good. We've only ever been able to injure it, and it's healed every time it returns. If you intend to attempt this, I wish you luck. Otherwise, go back where you came from and leave us alone."

Bobby watched their half-brother walk away,

annoyed the man couldn't even be bothered to offer his name. "Heckbiscuits," he muttered.

"I have no idea how to kill that dragon," Matthew said. "Or if we should even try."

"After meeting it, I can't imagine how we'd tame it either," Stephen said.

"We could go home and get some explosives," Jayce suggested. "Armor-piercing bullets. Rocket launchers?"

"Somehow, I suspect that kinda thing is gonna give these here elves the wrong idea about us."

"We just need to find something capable of cutting through its hide." Matthew sat on the flagstone path and leaned against the hedge. "If it's the same as your dragons, only bigger—"

"I don't think I'm gonna like whatever idea comes after that."

Jayce crouched and tapped the large, flat stone beside him, then he groped the edges like he wanted to pick it up. "Your dragons get smashed all the time. The metal isn't that strong in itself. It's just a matter of using enough force. That big dragon probably has thicker skin, so it's the difference between smashing one of your dragons and smashing me when I'm the same kind of metal, only times fifty."

"Yeah," Bobby grumbled, "all we need is a giant boot to come outta the sky and stomp on it. Then we'd be all set."

Stephen snorted. "Now there's a plan with no possibility of failure."

"Or success," Jayce added with a smirk. "Your dragons are actually mechanical, right?"

"Ayup." Bobby scuffed his shoe on the stone, trying to think. Coming up with a way to kill this dragon, though, amounted to coming up with a way to kill himself. He stuffed his hands in his pockets and shrugged. "They don't do well with tasers and that sorta thing."

"The elves already know that," Matthew said. "It explains the field around the settlement here. But it didn't seem to cause the dragon any real harm."

"Rung my bells, that's for sure. Also, they gotta eat metal. I ain't never figured out which kinds, I only know it ain't all kinds."

Stephen held up a hand and stared at nothing for a few seconds. "When your dragons get smashed, the other ones eat it, right? That is, more or less, how you regenerate. Right?"

"Ayup."

"And that dragon, did it eat some of yours?"

"I think so, sure."

Matthew's brow shot up. "That means your dragons could eat that dragon."

Bobby blinked at both men, long and slow. "Uh, they couldn't even scratch its eyes."

Jayce held out a hand. "Let me see one." After

Bobby popped one off his finger, it landed on his palm and Jayce held it up for a closer look. Stephen and Matthew leaned in. "The eyes aren't really different from the rest of it. Not significantly, anyway. They're probably as thick and tough as the skin."

"Look how thin the wings are, though." Stephen poked it and the dragon spread its wings out. "They're flimsy in comparison. Practically asking to be ripped off by an asshole little kid."

Already uncomfortable with the scrutiny and subject, Bobby squirmed. "Sebastian ain't no asshole kid." He turned his back on them when all three stared at him and it became clear Stephen hadn't meant that particular boy at all. "Anyway, this is…"

"The only way we're going to defeat that dragon," Stephen finished. "We have to attack the wings."

"Stephen will have to get it to open them," Matthew said. "Taunt it to fly at you. When it does, Bobby and I will attack while Jayce keeps it too distracted on the ground to chase Stephen. Jayce, do you think you could throw me onto its back?"

Jayce chuckled. "I've been wanting to try wolf tossing, but couldn't figure out how to ask without pissing you off."

"Good thing we got an opportunity for you," Bobby said with a roll of his eyes. "My part here is to eat the wings? Then dive in deeper and eat more?"

"And I'll back you up by ripping apart whatever I can," Matthew said.

"I sure heard worse plans. Heckbiscuits, I done come up with worse than that." Bobby jabbed a finger at Stephen and headed in the direction of the portal. "Don't you even start."

Stephen floated alongside him, smirking. "I wouldn't dream of it. C'mon. That dragon isn't going to eat itself."

"You know what? It didn't bother me that my dragons eat the ones what get broken until just now when you said that."

All three men laughed as they followed the signs of the giant dragon's passage. Though the creature hadn't left many full clawprints, Bobby found and stepped into one, thinking it would be funny. Instead, he shivered and hopped out. This thing had some kind of kinship to him, and he couldn't come up with a better plan to deal with it than killing it. No, worse—he meant to *eat* it.

Bobby resolved to make an effort to talk to the thing. Somehow. If he wanted to live with himself, he had to try.

Only a few dozen yards away, the dragon scraped at the ground with a front claw, tearing up small trees and flinging them aside. Bobby watched it, mesmerized by the raw, destructive power. His dragons could do incredible things, but not on the same scale. Beside him, Stephen, Jayce, and Matthew discussed details for approaching it in low whispers.

The minutia bored him. All four of them knew planning the details never worked. Paying them no attention, Bobby let his swarm peel off. Hundreds of tiny dragons darted to the giant dragon's head. They all shouted at once to get its attention. The giant dragon stopped digging.

Under Bobby's direction, the swarm trilled in unison to say they didn't want to hurt it. The giant dragon growled in the back of its throat. His swarm had no idea what it said. Unlike the elves, this dragon didn't share any sort of language with them by pure chance. While Bobby wondered how this made sense, the dragon reared and snapped at the swarm. Huge teeth crunched a dozen dragons while the rest of the swarm dispersed to attack the wings.

Twenty dragons still inside the mouth dove down its gullet. Bobby threw his mind into one of those dragons, certain the others could handle the command to eat the wings. The smooth outer skin masked joints using thousands of small gears and servos. Metal flaps snapped up and smacked tiny dragons, crunched and not, farther down the throat. Each flap tossed them deeper until they fell into a large cavity half-filled with sloshing liquid.

Already crushed dragons plopped into the liquid and sizzled. Bobby and the rest of the intact dragons hovered over the surface, watching in horrified fascination as the liquid bubbled and dissolved the tiny corpses. He now knew more about how his dragons worked than he ever wanted to.

They hit the sides and the liquid sloshed, suggesting the giant dragon must be running or jumping. Bobby led his demi-swarm up the tube but found it sealed. His dragon found an edge to dangle from and he realized the seal must flip open to let metal in. Since dragons could breathe fire, and fire came out of the mouth, the gasket had to block one while it shut the other.

Because they'd come here to eat this dragon, he wedged his jaws around the ledge and bit down. The tiny teeth had never dealt with metal this thick. He ground them against the surface, shaving thin strips away. With that minor success, the other dragons attacked anything they could wrap their mouths around. Screechy grinding filled the cavity.

The dragon moved again and the liquid heaved. Droplets showered the busy dragons, making them shriek with pain. One lost half its wing. Another had its tail dissolved. Bobby's hind leg fell off. They had to get out of this death trap. Urgency made the dragons gnaw faster and faster.

At the moment when several dragons chewed through holes too small to wriggle through, the flap snapped open. Every dragon leaped for freedom, then they attacked the gasket itself as it blocked the fire breath reservoir, devouring the edge with relish. Above, Bobby saw something falling toward them, pushed by the flinging flaps. Smashed tiny dragon corpses tumbled toward the stomach cavity. Though he hated to let them go, destroying the flap seemed more important than catching his crushed dragons. The hunks of twisted metal fell through the hole and splashed into the liquid. Bobby ducked aside as the gasket slapped down over the stomach again. The one-wing dragon didn't jump back fast enough to avoid being crunched.

Fire blasted from the other hole, taking Bobby by surprise and hurling him up. He tumbled in the fire until he saw daylight. Matthew the werewolf soared overhead and Jayce's shiny metallic form stood in the center of the flames on the ground, recovering from throwing Matthew. Above, Stephen hovered out of reach of the giant dragon's breath.

Bobby darted around the dragon to find the rest of his swarm. At least half, probably crunched by the dragon's wings, littered the ground around the giant dragon's feet. The rest attacked with angry fervor. Bobby joined them, refusing to think about what would happen when he re-formed his body.

Matthew hit the dragon's back and raked his claws across the folded wing with jarring metallic shrieks. The dragon reared with a defiant roar and shook its body. Thick claws lodged in the wing membrane, Matthew sailed through the air, back and forth, until the front wing bone snapped under his weight. He tore the membrane in half and dropped to the ground thirty feet below.

With only a few hundred dragons left, Bobby led the charge to eat away at the other wing. If it had responded to him, he'd feel bad about this. Instead, he dove into the job of devouring whatever his dragon could find. The tiny dragon bellies filled up, forcing them to spit the metal out. They filled the air with a silver shower.

The giant dragon screamed and loped away from Jayce. Stephen scooped up Matthew and followed. After only a few dragon-lengths of running, the dragon stopped again and flailed its front legs in the air. Jayce clung to one, his metallic sheen darker than the dragon's. Even while the dragon tried to shake him loose, the big man punched at the leg, denting it a tiny bit with every blow.

Stephen dropped Matthew on the back again and he grabbed the front edge of the other wing. With his own roar, he snapped the bone. Bobby's dragons had already cut through enough for it to rip the rest of the way. Matthew tossed it while the dragon bucked and jammed his claws into the joint on the dragon's back.

Fire filled Bobby's vision while he and his dragons attacked the other wing joint. Matthew screamed. His fur burning, he slid off the giant dragon's back. The dragon turned and reared, its front claws positioned to stomp the smoldering werewolf, even with Jayce still punching one.

"Hey, dragon!" Stephen shouted. "Yeah, you, the stupid silver thing! That's my brother!"

Bobby noticed Stephen floating to the side and saw him hurl a large rock at the dragon's head. It slammed into the dragon's face with a clunking thud and fell on Matthew. At least it helped the werewolf put the flames out, but he groaned with the crunching impact.

The dragon screeched in anger, its voice warped by the new dent in its snout. Bobby and his dragons broke through the outer layer of the joint and delved deeper, ripping, chewing, and grinding the wires and gears inside. Bobby chomped a thick wire and fought with it while the dragon danced and roared. Another of his dragons clamped onto the wire and helped him.

Electricity jolted both tiny dragons, causing their jaws to snap shut harder than they could manage on their own, which severed the wire and blew up the other tiny dragon. Bobby's dragon staggered into a pair of whirling gears, crunching its wingtip and dragging the whole body between them. Bobby's mind snapped out as his dragon was destroyed.

Now floating over the giant dragon's back, he took stock of the situation. Three dragons remained inside the gullet after the flaps tossed the rest back into the stomach cavity with too much force to recover. Outside the dragon, several more had been electrocuted at the other wing joint and still more had been dragged into gears, blown off course by fire to fall underfoot, smashed when Matthew fell, or hit by the second rock Stephen threw.

Bobby had thirty-three dragons left. He'd never lost so many at once. The idea of re-forming his body with so few terrified him. Would he be whole? If he wound up with only one dragon left… He panicked and ordered his dragons out. They had to retreat.

Jayce had punched a hole in the giant dragon's leg, and it now stumbled, from the inability to use both its foot and the joints Bobby had disabled. Stephen beat at his sleeve to put out the fire he hadn't fully dodged. Matthew, smoke rising from his singed fur, stood in front of the dragon. When it breathed fire at him, he rolled to the side and roared at it. The dragon lunged to bite Matthew and he sprang into its mouth.

Bobby had to help. He still had three on the inside. Picking one, he threw his mind into it and made a choice. The three dragons inside had gnawed enough around the edges of the gasket to wriggle out with minor damage to their wings. They crawled into the other tube, hoping to stop the fire before it hit Matthew.

Inside, he found a thin bar anchored at both ends of the six-inch high, smooth cavity. No gears or flaps worked here. Electricity crackled over the length of the bar. Behind it, a white mesh radiated enough heat to burn flesh. Behind that, a closed shutter blocked further passage. Bobby had no idea how this made billowing fire, but he could guess breaking one or more of these pieces would stop that.

Breaking this stuff would probably destroy these three dragons. While Bobby girded himself to sacrifice them, the shutter curled open and liquid shot through the mesh, then ignited on the bar. Flames erupted up the tube and Matthew screamed. The dragons needed no further encouragement. They knew what to do. Bobby tried to apologize as he tossed his mind out of the one dragon.

Thirty tiny dragons watched while the giant dragon's flames sputtered and died. Matthew's blackened claws punched through its neck and ripped the hole open wide enough for his charred, smoking body to fall out. With no more fire threatening him, Stephen darted in and gripped the dragon's head. He punched at its eye until his fist went through.

The giant dragon staggered and fell over, then Jayce and Stephen ripped it apart. Bobby landed the remains of his swarm on the dragon's shoulder and watched while Matthew groaned and didn't heal. As soon as the giant dragon stopped twitching, Stephen backed away from it, panting and holding his arm.

"My arm is burned," he grunted.

Matthew glared at him from the ground. Thin tendrils of smoke still drifted up from his once-furry body.

Stephen grinned weakly. "Where's Bobby?"

Bobby didn't want to re-form. Losing ten dragons made his hand hurt. Losing a few dozen made him hurt all the way to his shoulder. He still had no idea how it all worked and didn't want to find out. But he also couldn't sit here and pretend everything would be fine. Dragons wouldn't pop up out of thin air to join the swarm.

With a mental gulp, Bobby moved his dragons to the ground and ordered them to remake his body. Suddenly lying on the ground and wracked with pain, he squeezed his eyes shut and screamed. Someone picked him up and carried him, moving fast enough to jostle everything. Agony lanced through him from head to toe.

"Hold on, Bobby," Jayce said, his voice rumbling in his chest. Jayce set him down and lifted his hand with a finger under his wrist.

Warmth coursed through Bobby's body, chasing away a fraction of the agony. He opened his eyes in time to see shriveled petals fall to the ground. Jayce moved his hand to the next flower, and Bobby groaned as it healed him.

"I'm good for now." Bobby noticed blood all over his clothes. Thick lines of dark red stained his shirt and jeans all over.

"You're not bleeding from your eyes anymore. I'd say that's an improvement. There are more flowers, though. Are you sure you don't want to use them?"

"I'll live. We don't know what the plant needs to survive. Don't want to kill it by accident."

Jayce smirked. "No, we'll let Matthew do that. He's in bad shape too."

As if on cue, Stephen set Matthew on the ground beside them. He'd returned to his human form and now lay unconscious on the ground with bloody, charred flesh all over his body. They moved his hand to the plant and ran through three flowers before Matthew stirred. By then, his skin had healed, though it remained lobster-red.

"Fire bad," Matthew grunted.

"I hear that." Bobby sat up with a groan. "S'pose we oughta get that dragon's head and throw it on them elves' front lawn or something."

"I suggest we set up camp near the portal site first. You two get some rest. Stephen, stay with them. I'll take care of the head and the elves."

"Getting someone to sacrifice blood is probably asking too much," Stephen whined. "I'm starving now, and I'll be worse by the time the portal opens."

"We'll hold you back," Bobby said, meaning it. To Jayce, he said, "Don't punch nobody." He winced as he took Jayce's help to stand. Everything ached, but at least he could think. "Unless it's a dragon what ain't me."

Jayce chuckled.

Two and a half days of camping in a roomy tent near the portal site later, Bobby still ached all over. The four of them stood, waiting for the portal. Stephen's arm hadn't healed yet, and Matthew looked like a mildly undercooked lobster. It turned out that Jayce had dented his fist, which translated to broken fingers. When the elves complained about them using too many of the healing flowers, he'd turned to metal for the duration of their stay.

"These elves are dumb," Bobby said for the twenty-seventh time.

"We'll do our best for them." Jayce carried Bobby and Matthew's gear, as both still hurt too much for it.

"We should've asked to have a car waiting when we get back. With Liam in it." Matthew hadn't been able to regenerate. Werewolves, it seemed, didn't heal burns.

Stephen had sewn the charred fabric of his sleeve closed with clumsy stitches, but he still cradled his injured arm. Vampires didn't heal serious burns either. "Flying home is going to suck. Speaking of sucking, I'm incredibly hungry."

Before anyone could respond, the orange portal opened and Bobby dove through. He landed on his feet this time and kept going. The others followed him back into the lab. Stephen scanned the room and locked his gaze on the female lab assistant.

Bobby held a hand to block his sight. "You're too hungry for a room with only one lady in it."

Stephen sucked in a breath and nodded. "Thanks." He let Jayce hustle him away from her.

Dr. Eisenberg looked them over, his bright smile of excitement fading as he took in their condition. "I almost don't want to know what happened."

Jayce held up the pieces of the camera that had been destroyed in the dragon battle. "The memory card should be fine. Sorry about the damage."

"Report." General Hanstadt, the Chairman of the Joint Chiefs, stood to one side, hands clasped behind his back, uniform crisp, and black shoes polished. He seemed as fit, regimental, and unhappy to see them as ever.

Bobby handed Eisenberg the rest of the testing instruments they'd taken. Some survived intact. "Well, sir, we found a sentient race aware of humans and uninterested in dealing with you. They'll talk to us four in the future, but we're gonna have to take diplomacy real slow. There's some environmental hazards what your boys'd probably need nukes to deal with. If'n you decide to nuke that world—"

"I'm familiar with your brand of threats." Hanstadt waved Bobby off. "We'll review the data and decide if your further involvement would be beneficial."

"I had a feeling you might say something like that." Bobby had stewed over how to respond to this for two days. If he destroyed the portal device, they'd take their notes and build a new one, probably bigger and better than this one. He'd practically be doing them a favor. "Don't worry, we ain't gonna blow nothing up. Instead, I'll just point out that now we know it's possible, ain't gonna be long before we can make our own portal."

To his satisfaction, Hanstadt's face tightened and his brow furrowed. "I'll keep that in mind."

With a curt nod, Bobby led the way out of the room. As he stalked through the halls, he caught sight of Mike, their contact here. He wanted to pass along a message without Mike's bosses knowing anything. In a flash of brilliance, he grabbed Mike's polo shirt sleeve. "You, I'm all turned around in these hallways. Show us the way out."

"Uh, sure." Mike gulped and blinked, then he pointed in the right direction. "You're that spokesdragon guy, right?"

Letting go of Mike's shirt, Bobby nodded and let him set the pace. "Yessir, I surely am. What's your job here?"

"Computer stuff. Probably boring compared to a

superhero."

"I dunno. Could be real interesting when stuff is going on here."

"I suppose." Mike glanced behind them at the other three men and blinked some more. "Oh. Yes. You're right. Whenever the bigwigs show up, it's always interesting around here."

"Interesting is always interesting." Bobby had no idea what else to say in his effort to convey his message to contact them if he heard about any other official visits, portal use, or other shady business.

"Sure. I get that." He pointed at the door ahead. "That's the way out. Have a safe trip." Flashing two thumbs up, he raised his brow with a smile. "Probably see you again soon."

Bobby nodded and clapped the guy on the arm. They breezed past the guards outside and into the warm, sunny afternoon. Taking a deep breath of Earth air, he noted it smelled different, though he had trouble putting a word to it. Used, maybe, or less alive.

"Smooth, Bobby." Stephen smacked him in the back, which hurt like heckbiscuits. "We could've gotten a ride home, but you had to shoot off your mouth again. It's like a talent."

"He wasn't going to offer us a ride anyway," Jayce said.

"The sun is so harsh here it hurts," Matthew

growled. "Let's get out of here."

"Welcome to my world." Stephen snorted. "I'm not going far without eating."

Bobby shrugged. "We can hit Albuquerque on the way back."

"Just don't forget to take the left." Jayce grinned as he turned into his windbreaker.

With a deep breath, Bobby let his swarm peel off, amazed he now had hundreds of dragons again. The swarm still seemed only about half its usual size, which explained why he still felt like crap. He picked up Jayce while Stephen hoisted Matthew onto his back and the foursome flew away.

Hours later, they landed at the farm under the setting sun. Matthew whimpered as a well-fed Stephen set him down in the shade. Bobby re-formed and grinned as Sebastian burst through the front door, blue frosting smudged on his cheeks. The boy leaped at Bobby, who caught him with a grunt and wince.

Sebastian squeezed him around the neck harder than Bobby could stand. Blissfully unaware of the agony he put Bobby through, he giggled. "Where's my present?"

Settling the kid on his hip, Bobby forced himself to maintain his grin. "What, I ain't enough?"

The boy's face fell into a pout. "You *promised*."

"Okay, okay. Here." Bobby retrieved a silver gear he'd liberated from the giant dragon's corpse and held it up. "This here is from the place we went. A giant robot monster tried to eat us. We all done got banged up, but we took care of it so it won't hurt no one else."

Sebastian held the gear up and peered at Bobby. His gaze bored into Bobby's skull, making him feel like the kid could read his thoughts. Sliding the gear onto his thumb, he smiled and pointed at the house. "Cake. Sam made it. No kale."

"Sounds good." Bobby carried the kid inside, satisfied that cake—followed by a visit with their healer—made the best possible end to this fiasco.

Sechin Tower is a writer and a teacher. A life-long gamer, he began his professional writing career in 2006 as an editor for Exile Game Studio and went on to become the chief contributor to the *Hollow Earth Expedition RPG*'s award-winning game supplements. He lives in the Seattle, WA area with his beautiful wife and noisy cat. In his spare time, he prepares for the zombie apocalypse by running obstacle courses and playing way too many video games.

The Chupacabra and the Dragon

SECHIN TOWER

I. The Chupacabra

The reek of the human's perfume stings my nose so badly that I can barely detect the bright tingling scent of the gunpowder in their weapons.

I hide. If I were to stand upright, I would be almost as tall as the humans and they would surely see me against the backdrop of the starry sky. Instead, I lay on my belly and relax my dorsal quills down to my spine. Then I shift the color of my skin from its usual gray to the reddish-yellow hue of the sandy dirt beneath my claws.

There are two humans, one male and one female. The female wears the perfume. They scramble from their car with the quick, sloppy movements of scavengers who have discovered a carcass too big for them to defend. They do not know I am here, so something else must be triggering their fear instinct.

I watch. The male, who smells only of the pungent body odor of his species, tucks a weapon into his belt and hurries around to the rear of the car. When he opens the trunk, the spicy tang of fear blooms into the desert night. This is why they are afraid: they have another human in the trunk. I can smell that this one is a child. A frightened child.

From their behavior, I would guess that these two child-thieves have transgressed against their herd by imprisoning this child in their trunk. But I do not understand why they would risk reprisal from their own kind in this way. Are they planning to eat their captive? I've never known humans to do this, but their inconsistent cruelty often surprises me. I would understand if they were always cruel, for nature often requires aggressive behavior. I would also understand if they were always kind, for I have seen these hairless apes accomplish tremendous feats through cooperation. What baffles me is the way they switch between the two so easily. How do they select the targets of their cruelty and the recipients of their friendship? I have no answer.

Humans have always made me so curious. Perhaps I am drawn to them because I have not yet found any members of my own species, despite my searching. Maybe if I understood more about myself, I would be less interested in the complicated and incomprehensible interactions of humankind. Until I find another like me, however, these ungainly bipedal mammals remain the only creatures that I find both interesting and frightening.

I decide to follow these two child-thieves as they haul their small captive toward a darkened wooden dwelling. They have bound the child at the wrists and ankles with strips of a durable fabric covered on one side by very sticky chemicals. Humans call it *duct tape*. The child thrashes fiercely, but this does little to slow their progress. He attempts to wail, but a patch of tape covers his mouth and mutes his noise.

"This is a bad idea," the male child-thief says.

"Shut up and get the door," the female hisses.

My mouth cannot produce their sounds, but I have learned to understand the speech of humans. I have also come to understand that these creatures are practically blind, deaf, and otherwise unable to clearly perceive their surroundings. They seem not to hear or smell what is obvious to me, and I am beginning to suspect that they cannot even see the red light of heat radiating from living bodies. For these reasons, I know I am safe even inches away from them, at least while we are in the dark.

I slide over the desert on all fours until I am at their heels. I am close enough to slice the tendons behind their ankles if I wished. The female's head swings around, but she looks right over me without even guessing that I exist. Humans would make wonderful prey, if only they didn't taste so awful.

Fortunately, these two enter their darkened house through a sliding door. I cannot turn doorknobs with my claws, and this makes it very difficult for me to move about human habitats. Sliding doors, however, are easy to push open. In this case, the humans are so intent on carrying the child to the far side of the house that they don't even lock it behind them. While they move down the hallway and out of sight, I hook a claw onto the handle and pull the door along its track.

The repulsive scent of perfume rolls over me. I close my nostrils, but it is too late: the intense stink has left me temporarily nose-blind. If I enter the house, I will do so without the benefit of one of my keenest senses. It takes a moment for my curiosity to win out over my discomfort.

I hunger. The kitchen contains a large white box called a refrigerator, and this is where food is stored. I can hear the two adults carrying the child to a room in the far side of the dwelling, so I know I have time to slide my claws through the magnetic material lining the refrigerator door. I tear it a little as I open it, but not too badly. Inside, there is half of an old pizza in a grease-stained box, a lump of ground cow meat wrapped in a transparent polymer sheet, and a duffel bag containing several pounds of explosively flammable chemicals. I reach for the cow meat.

I eat. I have never seen a cow, but from the taste of their meat I have determined they are large, four legged herbivores with a ruminant stomach system. They seem so defenseless—and delicious—that they must be the result of centuries of selective breeding. I can read all of this and more in the taste of the meat. I can do this with any animal or plant that I taste, although I do not understand how I do this any more than I understand how my nose interprets chemical compounds as scents. All I know is that my ancient ancestors, those of the species that created the genetic blueprint from which I was cloned, were masters of genetic alteration. They must have designed me with the ability to read DNA by tasting it. Certainly, this is a useful hunting talent, because once I capture an animal I know how other members of its species behave, how they will defend themselves, and where to find them.

I barely have time to swallow the lump of meat before the human child-thieves walk back toward this end of the dwelling. They are turning on lights as they approach, and I cannot hide well in bright light.

"I'm just saying it's not nice to call the kid a retard," the male speaks in a whining tone as he approaches the kitchen. "You're not supposed to use that word anymore."

"Then what the hell am I supposed to call the little retard?" the female barks from the front room.

"For one thing," the male says. "This one's not retarded. It's Down's Syndrome."

"Down's Syndrome is a kind of retarded, ain't it?"

"For another thing," the male goes on. "You're supposed to say it's a person with a bad thing instead of calling them by the bad thing. I mean, like: 'the kid *with* Down's Syndrome' instead of 'he's a Down's Syndrome kid.' It's just polite."

"Politeness ain't exactly our main concern here, considering that we snatched the little retard from the sidewalk while his mom was two steps away."

This is the end of the conversation. It is clear she is the alpha in this relationship.

The male sighs and flips on the kitchen light. I am crouched behind the countertop island, two feet away from him. Cornered.

He takes a step toward the refrigerator. I can sense his position by listening to his footsteps and watching the orange-yellow heat that radiates from his body. If he leaned over far enough, he would look right down at me. But he doesn't lean, and he doesn't look. Instead, he bends down to lift the empty plastic wrapper from the meat I just consumed. I hear it crinkle in his fingers as he grunts in mild confusion. Then he places the wrapper onto the countertop and proceeds toward the refrigerator. As he moves, I circle around the counter in the opposite direction.

"I told her we should stick to torching buildings for insurance money," he mumbles to himself as he adjusts the duffel bag of chemicals on the bottom shelf. His keeps his voice too quiet for the female to hear. "Less dangerous, I said. Less messy, too. But does she listen? Oh, no, we need to kidnap a billionaire retard."

While he occupies himself with his complaints, I slink out of the kitchen and into the hallway. I am out of the line of sight of the male, but now in plain view of the front room. Fortunately, the female is hunched over a stack of magazines at a table, her back to me. She is cutting out individual letters from the printed words and piling them in a nice, neat stack next to a bottle of white glue.

I dart down the hallway and sniff out the room where they have imprisoned the child. I am lucky: they have left the door ajar so I am able to enter.

The room is dimly lit by a small electric bulb in a floor socket. There are stacks of old clothes in one the corner, and the child sits in the other. He has been duct-taped to a mattress. I see the salty tears that streak his face. I hear his whimpering. Even over the perfume, I smell the ammonia in the urine that has stained his pants.

His eyes are open. He stares at me.

Usually, humans scream when they see me, particularly if I forget to lower the long quills which protrude from my back and elbows. Yet this child displays no fear reaction. In fact, I hear his heartbeat slow a little, and I think I detect a smile beneath the tape on his mouth.

I cock my head.

Perhaps in imitation of me, he cocks his head.

Curious, I move closer. I am careful to keep my teeth hidden and my claws curled under my palm. I want to appear as nonthreatening as possible. Trapped as he is, my approach would trigger panic in most humans, but not in him.

I examine. I am not familiar with the words which the child-thieves used to describe their prisoner. They seemed to think he is special in some way. To me, all humans are so alike that I have not yet worked out classifications for them. I was created in a laboratory by a scientist who had discovered an ancient genetic blueprint engineered by my ancestors. I was created from that blueprint. That scientist is now dead, but before I escaped from him I learned many things by watching and listening. I learned that the world is round and vast and that humans breed in inconceivable numbers everywhere on its surface. Some humans have different color hair and skin, but even the starkest external contrasts represent very small genetic differences compared to other animals.

The child has a scrape on his wrist next to the tape, so I carefully, gently lick it. I can taste that he has one extra chromosome compared to other members of his species, but the implications are too complex for me to understand how this would affect him. To me, he appears to be the same as any other human.

Again I wonder what the child-thieves want with this child. Based on their conversation, it seems unlikely that they were going to eat him, as I first supposed. Perhaps this child, being in a special classification for whatever reason, gives them permission to be cruel to him. Perhaps his mother has offended them in some way. Yet no matter how many explanations I think up, I cannot find one that satisfies all the questions about their behavior.

I am five summers old and I do not yet understand human beings. I must be a slow learner.

The child continues to study me as I study him. I would like to hear what he has to say, but if I attempted to remove the tape from his mouth I would surely cut his face with my claws. Instead, I slice through the bonds on his wrists and arms. Immediately, he pulls the tape from his own mouth. This takes time and seems to cause pain as the adhesive pulls at his skin. His heart rate accelerates. Then he looks at me and calms back down. With his right hand, he reaches up to feel the side of my face. I try not to flinch at the clammy smoothness of human fingers touching my pebbled skin. He smiles. I flick my tongue toward him and chirp a few calming notes.

A scream bursts from the open doorway behind

me. It is the sound of unfiltered, unrestrained terror. It is the typical human reaction to seeing me.

I spin around to see the male child-thief standing in the doorway, hands up defensively, legs spread wide, knees wobbling slightly. I have clearly triggered his fear instinct.

If I had not been nose-blind from the perfume and concentrating so intently on the child, I might have sensed him coming and hidden myself from his view. Instead, I must shove past him and gallop down the hallway, hoping to escape the way I came in.

"Alligator! Alligator!" I hear the male screaming.

The female doesn't answer, but from the front room I hear the heavy metallic clicking of a weapon.

I am almost outside when the sound of a gunshot explodes around me. The bullet misses, but my ears ring painfully and the glass door in front of me explodes into glittering fragments. This saves me the trouble of breaking it for myself. I leap through the shards into the night air.

Outside, lights flick on in the surrounding dwellings. Behind the curtains and windows, I can see the orange heat signatures of human bodies rising from their beds. They reach for their phones to spread the message of alarm within their settlement.

I know I cannot stand in the middle of the dirt lot behind the house, and I cannot run fast enough to reach cover before the female steps through the door and opens fire. Therefore, I leap to the top of the car, then backward to the side of their dwelling. I lock my claws over my palm to make them into tree-climbing hooks. A house made from wood is not so different from a tree, so I am able to stick to the siding like a fly on a wall.

The female emerges into the back yard, her weapon raised to her shoulder. When I scamper up the side of the house, she spins to face me. Too late I realize that my claws make noise as they dig into the siding. My ears still ring from the previous gunshot and so I cannot hear well, but humans, whose hearing is so poor to begin with, seem to have no trouble.

I hear three shots behind me. One bullet hole opens in the side of the house, five inches from my nose, but I swing over the roof line and drop down into the side yard before I am hit.

Through the chinks in the wooden fence, I see the female approaching the side yard, her body and the barrel of her weapon both burning red in the cool night. She will spot me in only a moment. Beside me is the window to the room where they keep the captured child. I leap through it, feeling the glass scrape me as I break it.

The child watches as I roll to the floor in front of him.

I have only a moment to decide what to do with him. If I had longer, I might make a rational choice. Instead, I slit the child's remaining bonds and scoop him up in my arms. I carry him through the door just as the female shoots through the window into the room. The little light bulb, the room's only light source, explodes and goes dark.

Once again, I find myself bounding down the hallway. Ahead of me, the male child-thief emerges from the kitchen, the duffel bag of chemicals slung over his shoulder and a steel knife clutched in his hand. The blade is longer than my claws and probably sharper, and it glints wickedly in the artificial light.

With the child still in my arms, I leap directly at the male.

I am thin and lanky, while the human, as a typical member of a species closely related to gorillas, is thick-bodied and heavy-footed. He could easily have planted his feet to absorb my momentum, or else held that knife in front of him and allowed me to impale myself. But he is startled and, I judge, of timid character, so he is already falling backward by the time I drive my shoulder into him. He tumbles to the ground, and I continue my mad dash for the exit.

I am about to run back out the window, but I can see that the female has entered the car and now sits behind the steering wheel. She sees me and lifts her weapon from the passenger seat. Before she can aim, I sprint back into the house.

I cannot move quickly on two feet, so I tuck the

child under one of my arms and do my best to gallop on three legs. The male adult is still on the floor, curled into a ball around his duffel bag. This makes it easy to leap over him as I go. In the front room, I knock over the table with the magazines. The cut-out letters flutter about me like snow. Then I break through the front window and am free.

I run only as far as the center of the street. All the dwellings around me are lit brightly. Dozens of humans peer out of their windows at me. A few have even ventured out on their dusty front lawns. Many aim their phones at me.

I throw my arm over my face just in time to protect my eyes from a bright camera flash. When I blink my eyes open, I see one human has aimed a weapon at me.

Just before he can fire, another human seizes his arm and says "Don't! You might hit the kid!"

A roar and a splintering crash startle me. The female child-thief has smashed through the fence with her car and now hurtles out onto the street. The headlights glare like the eyes of a predator.

She means to run me down. Clearly, unlike the other humans, she is unconcerned about "hitting the kid."

I gather the child to my chest. An instant before the car collides with us, I leap as high as I can. The vehicle whizzes beneath me. I feel its metal skin scrape the claws of my hind feet. If the car were moving less quickly, I would have landed on it, but its speed is great enough to carry it past me before I land.

Tires squeal. The vehicle cannot turn sharply enough. With a crash as loud as a gunshot, it slams into a yellow metal plug known as a fire hydrant. The vehicle's front window shatters to a storm of glass, and the female child-thief is launched through it, head first. In that same instant, a geyser erupts from the broken fire hydrant and this, combined with the vehicle's remaining momentum, knocks the car onto its side and sends it skidding into a house.

For an instant, all human eyes turn toward the wreck. This gives me just enough time to hop over a nearby fence. Already, I hear the piercing wail of sirens moving down the streets toward us, but I will not be here when those sirens arrive.

Humans expect everyone to move along their paved roads, which is why I travel at a diagonal. I need to cut through only eight yards to escape the area where the herd is on high alert, and after that the journey is easy. I trigger a few automatic backyard lights, but I avoid the yards where I smell dogs and otherwise find no difficulty in escaping notice. It helps that I have the ability to hold my body heat within myself for short periods of time, which is useful for remaining invisible to snakes and infrared cameras. I was designed for stealth, and no creature I have ever met can match me in this.

The child remains silent as we travel. I hug him to

my chest beneath me to shield him from view, and he seems to relax within this constraint. I do not understand why the child-thieves felt entitled to be cruel to him, so I decide not to abandon him until I can be sure that other humans will not mistreat him in a similar way.

Soon, I—we—escape from the human settlement into the desert. Here I am, about to rest and consider what to do with this child when I catch a displeasingly familiar scent. It is the bitter aroma of flammable chemicals. I have stumbled across the trail of the male child-thief.

This introduces a new possibilities. If I track him down, I might devise a way to get him to speak about what he and the female had intended to do with their prisoner, and this might allow me to better understand what to do with the child. Therefore, I scoop the child up once more and head out after my new quarry, careful to drag my tail behind me to erase my tracks as I walk.

Behind a small hillock, the chemical scent comes to an end. The man's body odor continues on, but he seems to have left the chemicals behind. I run my claws through the dirt and find that it has been freshly disturbed.

I dig. Three feet down, I find the duffel bag with the explosives. Buried at this depth, it would stay cool even under the hot sun while also remaining safely hidden, at least from other human eyes.

I have no use for these chemicals, so I re-bury the

duffel bag. As I do, the child sits, chews on the side of his thumb, and stares at me.

Again, I gather him in my arms. He clings to my neck. I am reminded of images of primates, the closest genetic relatives to human beings, and how their young hang on their parents. Human beings are not so different from their ancestors as they seem to think. This thought also raises an important question: does this child consider me a parent? Does he understand that I saved him from cruelty and, in his innocent simplicity, does he therefore trust me implicitly? I find it odd that he does not vocalize his feelings as the other members of his species seem unable to stop doing, but perhaps he is too young for verbal expression.

With the child under one arm, I lope deeper into the desert. Tracking the child-thief is easy, and soon his scent grows very strong. I expect he is just past the next hillock, and a lack of sound indicates that he has ceased moving.

A breeze carries the tangy iron scent of blood. I frieze in place. The child whimpers; perhaps he senses something, too.

I sniff. The odor of blood is mixed with the itchy scent of venom. Venom like a rattlesnake's, but it smells more deadly. I lower myself as close to the ground as I can while holding the child tight to my chest. Silently, I creep forward to peer over the hillock.

What I see makes no sense.

The human is dead, that much is obvious. Minor wounds ooze blood from his neck, hands, and forearms, and the stench of venom is now strong enough to burn my nostrils. Whatever bit or stung him must have injected a toxin that stopped his heart mere minutes ago, because his body is still warm and his eyes still stare up at the sky. His sharp knife lays in the dirt only a few inches from his limp fingers.

What confuses me is the army of assorted vermin that has descended on him not to eat him, but to transport him. A massive flotilla of ants marches beneath him, carrying him on their collective backs. At the same time, a troop of rats takes turns seizing his clothing and pulling him forward, lending their strength to the ant's effort. The ants do not attack the rats, the rats do not eat the ants, and neither group has taken a single bite of the corpse. Together, they glide the body toward a dark, sandy hole that looks just wide enough to swallow the entire procession.

What I am seeing is clearly unnatural. Each of these species, the rats and the ants, are aggressive scavengers that compete for the same food sources. There is no precedent for a symbiotic relationship any more than there is a history of such creatures attacking a healthy human who outweighs all of them put together.

I should flee. I know this. And yet, while the voice

of fear sings loudly to me, the voice of hope whispers that my long search has finally ended. There is only one species that could have caused what I am seeing. My species.

The flapping of feathers startles me. I leap backward and spin around, almost dropping the child as I do. Before me, a buzzard settles onto the hillock, his long wings dropping to his sides and his neck folding into a smug curve.

Buzzards are not nocturnal, yet this scavenging bird stares at me intently through the dim moonlight as if I, not he, am out of place.

"The Dragon speaks through me," the buzzard chirps. Yes, chirps: he does not utter the coarse calls of his kind, but rather speaks the twittering language that immediately forms meaning in my mind. I recognize it as the language of my own species. I was born with it built into my brain, a genetic program as much a part of me as my tail and claws. Even so, I have never before heard the words come from any throat other than my own.

"Are you… are you The Dragon?" I ask. It is not impossible that a member of my species would take the shape of a buzzard. Their mastery of DNA manipulation would allow them to assume any form they wished.

"The Dragon speaks through me," the buzzard repeats. "The Dragon awaits below. What is it that you seek?"

So, this buzzard is a mere servant. A thrall, like the

ants and rats. But the master is nearby.

I can feel the quills stand upright all along my spine. After searching for so long, I am paralyzed in the presence of that which I have sought. I look at the hole in the ground and see that the ants and the rats have already transported the child-thief's body inside, and his feet are now disappearing into the darkness.

The human child whimpers in my arms. I find myself unable to form words.

"Be gone, then," the buzzard says, a throaty squawk adding an edge to his words.

"Wait," I say. "The—ah—The Dragon. Please tell him that I seek… I seek his wisdom. I have come to learn of our species."

The buzzard pauses, half-crouched, and gazes at me. His eyes are black beads inside a skull. Without another word, he extends his wing to point toward the tunnel where the ants and rats have carried their prize.

I hesitate. Something churns in my stomach.

The child stirs and I wonder if he, too, may sense danger. Still, he makes no sign of struggle as I crouch down and slide into the mouth of the tunnel. Inside, it is so narrow that I could not turn around if I wanted to. I can only move forward, toward the only thing I have ever truly desired—and the only thing I have ever truly feared.

II. The Dragon

I descend.

The deeper I go, the more I must struggle against my fear instinct. My only reassurance is that if The Dragon wished to kill me, he would already have collapsed the tunnel onto my head or attacked me from the rear, where I could not defend myself in such a small space.

I wonder if The Dragon is as curious about me as I am about him. This is a distressing thought, because it could mean he has nothing to teach me about my species. Even at the risk of my life, there is much that I hope to learn. I do not even know my own life cycle. How long will I live? How can I expect my body to age, and what diseases or infirmities must I avoid? I do not even know why my species disappeared from this Earth so many millions of years ago. I am willing to risk my life for a chance at answers.

The narrow tunnel stretches on for hundreds of paces before it opens into a larger system of caverns. Here, the walls are speckled with bioluminescent fungus that glows so faintly even I can barely see by its light. At each intersection within the snaking passages, I gouge the walls with my claws to indicate my path, and then I continue to follow the faint trail of heat left by the rats, the ants, and the body they carry.

The child breathes heavily and seems to be asleep. No—not asleep. I sniff his neck and find a red welt forming on his jugular that smells icy and tingling. He has been poisoned, made comatose by a paralytic toxin. This toxin could have been delivered by an insect at any time since we entered the tunnel, and there is no way I could have foreseen it or prevented it.

A rat scampers out of a hole up to a small dirt ledge that brings him almost eye-to-eye with me. He is large by the standards of his kind, and his coat is thick and glossy.

"The Dragon speaks through me," the rat chirps in my language. "The Dragon has been courteous enough to allow your meal to live."

By "meal," he must be referring to the child. It is a reasonable assumption for why I would be carrying a member of another species under my arm.

"The Dragon poisoned this the child?" I ask.

"Not poisoned—preserved. The child will sleep for a day and his meat will be as fresh as it is now. The Dragon will allow you to keep him. This is a gift to you."

"I speak to you now, rat," I say. "Why do you serve The Dragon?"

"The Dragon speaks through me," the rat says.

"How is it that you can use the language of my species?"

"The Dragon speaks through me."

No matter what other questions I ask, the answer is always the same. It seems an automatic response, leading me to believe that the rat cannot truly understand my words or respond intelligently. It delivers messages as a mindless, automatic behavior, no doubt a simple expression of genetic tampering by its master.

I leave the rat behind and travel thousands of paces deeper into these underground passages, until solid stone caverns replaces the earthen tunnels. Everywhere, the passages are alive with countless small insects, reptiles, and mammals, all behaving in ways that run counter to their usual nature. Beetles patch walls with new stones. Burrowing termites dig new tunnels large enough for me to pass through. Rats and lizards march past me with scraps of food clutched in their jaws, yet not eating. Snakes sit coiled at intersections, no doubt ready to guard against intruders. This underground cavern complex is not an ecosystem, it is an organism—a single living being divided into many bodies, most of which mindlessly provide nourishment and information to its central occupant.

My dorsal quills shiver as I wonder what my species has evolved into over the countless eons. Whatever it is, I am about to find out.

I continue. Still following the main troop of ants and rats, I arrive at a jagged rip in a stone wall. This opening is widest on the bottom, where the ants and rats have no trouble carrying the corpse through to the dark hollow beyond.

Peering in, I wonder if I have gone blind. There is no heat, no smell, and no sound. I feel nothing but a faint, intermittent air current from within.

The earth beneath me rumbles in a frequency so low I feel it in the pads of my feet more than hear it with my ears. This noise is a voice that is so deep and ancient that it has almost become part of the Earth itself.

"I smell you," the voice from within the hollow speaks. As it does, teeth flash in the dark, revealing the speaker to be much closer and much larger than I had imagined.

My skin crawls as if it were trying to flee without me. I cannot speak.

"You wear a primitive body," the voice says. "Mountains have risen and fallen since I have smelled a body of your type. Two hundred million summers, more or less."

Two hundred million summers. My mind cannot grasp this span of time. Could any living creature be so old? If my ancestors truly perfected genetic engineering, then immortality would have been possible, but the sheer weight of the ages threatens to compress me into nothingness.

"You—you—" I stammer. "How could you have survived for so long?"

"Survival is easy," the words come in a slow gust of wind. "Remembering… remembering is difficult. Would you like to remember the long eons with me?"

"I cannot remember," I say. "I was not there."

"How little you know of your own potential. Set down the human hatchling and enter my den."

I gently place the child against the cavern wall. Then I step through, into the hollow. I cannot determine the size of this inner cavern because I cannot see the walls and the room's echoes are baffled by numerous rough pillars formed by mineral accretion. The only heat comes from a large pool of something that is not water, and I see a steady stream of small animals depositing their scraps of food into this pool, like ants paying homage to their queen.

Before I can ask what this liquid is, I am disturbed by the grisly sounds of cracking bones. The human corpse, I know, is the source of the sounds.

"Humans are salty and rank," The Dragon growls with mild distaste. "Yet they provide such a wonderful variety of waste food to scavenge. But I ask you: do you not intend to eat that human hatchling you carried here?"

I do not answer. I still cannot see The Dragon, not even his body heat. I can hold my body heat within me, but it is uncomfortable and I cannot do it for more than a few minutes at a time. The Dragon must find it far easier than I do.

"I ask again," The Dragon says. "What will you do with that human hatchling?"

"I intend to return it to its mother," I say, finally finding my voice.

"Why not eat it?"

"Some humans have been kind to me," I say. "I know from experience that it is possible to live symbiotically with them. Perhaps this one will grow into such a relationship with me. And…"

"And?"

"And I have observed that these creatures care deeply for their young. I would spare this one's mother the emotional pain of losing her child."

"Weakness," The Dragon spits, and something metallic hits the far wall. I think it may have been the child-thief's belt buckle. "Long ago, our species suffered from the need for companionship. We had complex relationships, all stemming from the need to produce and raise young. But immortality means not suffering the burden of needing offspring, and not needing offspring means not needing others. We fixed ourselves—those of us who survived. Those who didn't, died. You must truly wear an inferior body if you still suffer from a need for companionship. How very pitiable, considering that all your potential companions died eons ago."

I am stunned. I am saddened. I grapple with the realization that The Dragon is correct: I am an outdated creature born millions of years too late. I wonder what it would be like to alter my body to eliminate my desire for companionship, but I will never know.

As the words sink in, the only sound is the distant clicking of insect legs in the tunnels around us.

"You seem to understand these humans." The Dragon breathes. "As you have seen, I can create many different creatures. Birds, rodents, even bacteria—I grow them from my own body and they all function properly. Yet I have not been able to create a fully functional human, even though I have often tasted their life essence."

"Their interactions are complex," I say. "I do not fully understand them. Sometimes, I think they do not understand themselves."

"I want to know more," The Dragon announces. "I want to understand their technology as well. And you— you want to befriend them, but surely you understand that they would react violently to you. Even if you return this hatchling, they are more likely to offer you hostility than symbiosis."

"I am willing to take that risk."

"I have a gift for you, then," The Dragon speaks with such immediacy that I wondered how long he has been waiting to say this. "Step closer, toward the pool. Stand on the edge there and all shall be made clear."

The pool stretches before me like a smooth, glassy floor. I squat down to sniff it, and as soon as I do, ripples spread out before me. Whatever this liquid is, it is thick, like tree sap, and it smells oddly familiar.

"What is this?" I ask.

"Memory," The Dragon answers.

I look in his direction and catch only a glint of red eyes.

"What do you know of the mechanisms of life?" The Dragon asks. "Do you know of the tiny filaments that contain each creature's living essence?"

I think for a moment. "I was born in a human science laboratory," I say. "I think I know what you are describing. Humans call it DNA."

It is difficult to pronounce the human word in the sing-song language of my species, but the meaning is clear enough.

The Dragon's red eyes narrow, but I cannot read his emotion.

"So, the humans have discovered the secret," he rumbles. "Their ability must still be in its infancy, while my ancestors—our ancestors—used the threads of living essence to re-weave the entire world. I would tell you of this, but speech is such a poor vessel. Instead, you should drink. Drink, and all will be explained."

I am confused. I look back at the pool of not-water and stare in wonder as the surface ripples and distends toward me. At first, it seems that a creature is arising from its depths, but it is the liquid itself that is shifting, defying gravity to draw itself up into a small mound. The tip of this distortion supports a single drop, poised as if to fall upward toward the ceiling.

"Drink, and you shall share part of my experience," The Dragon says. "When my—our—ancestors discovered the means to create eternal life, they knew they would need to create eternal memories as well. After a mere few centuries, a living brain becomes too jumbled to recall events swiftly, and so we created memory pools such as this. It stores memories inside the threads of essence."

My breath catches in my throat. If I understand him correctly, this pool contains two hundred million years of conscious awareness, all encoded in DNA—or "threads of essence," as he calls them. DNA is nature's original memory system, and to use it to record thoughts and impressions would be no great leap from what humans have already accomplished. If this pool truly contains The Dragon's lifetime of experience, then it holds eye-witness accounts of at least two mass extinctions, as well as the answers to countless questions about life on Earth that human scientists have been pursuing since the dawn of their species.

"But what good will this drop do me?" I ask. "I cannot share the memory you offer. Even if I drink it, I will know nothing about you except, perhaps, your flavor."

"Can you really be so ignorant of yourself?" the tone is casually derisive. "You are an early attempt at improving upon nature, and you are far inferior to me. Even so, you are not without some rudimentary abilities. You were designed with a heightened perception of threads of essence. Are you not aware of this when you eat?"

I consider what he is saying. He must be referring to my ability to learn a creature's appearance and behavior from sampling their meat or blood. I had always suspected that this represented some kind of ability to read genetic information, but I never imagined that it could be used as a form of communication.

"Your ability to taste the threads of essence is rudimentary, of course," The Dragon continues. "When I taste, I know the entire tale of that creature's heritage and all its ancestors, stretching back to The Beginning. And I record it as a memory, should I wish to grow creatures of its sort. You, however, likely understand nothing more than the most obvious expressions, but this will still allow you to participate in my memories, so long as I encode them in the proper way."

I look at the upside-down teardrop that holds the memory. Fear dances along my spine, and I must remind myself that if The Dragon wanted me dead, I would be so already.

Prostrating myself before the pit, I can just reach the drop with the tip of my tongue. It flows into my mouth, and for a moment I feel nothing. I begin to wonder if I am too flawed to understand what I have been given.

Then the world is changed. It grips me, as sudden and as disorienting as a hurricane. This knowledge does not feel like listening to a story with a beginning and an ending, but rather like my self-awareness has been ripped open and an entirely new life has been shoved inside. I was born only five summers ago, but this memory has expanded my experience by millennia—or, at least, by pieces of millennia, knitted together not by linear time but by experiential connections.

As the memories shatter the borders of my self-perception, I struggle to separate my identity from The Dragon's. For a time, I fail. It is as if I hatched twice, grew twice, and developed into two distinct individuals. One version of my life began in a human laboratory, but the other started eons ago.

I have The Dragon's very earliest memory, that of emerging from the egg. It seems to be my own tooth which cuts through the shell, my own tiny lungs that take in the first gasp of air. I am he; he is me. This version of me was born with a purpose. I am a new breed of warrior and survivalist, engineered for unlimited power and adaptability—and yet as a hatchling I am small and weak, without any understanding of the world save that there is an enemy which wants to destroy me. I find myself alone in a cavern, and thunder shakes dirt from the ceiling and makes my feet slip on the slick fluid from my egg. My first sensation is that of fear.

Later, I look back on this as the era of the invasion, the moment when my species comes closest to extinction. I do not encounter The Invaders until years later, when I am fully grown and capable of engaging them in battle. They are creatures of metal and crystal, and they fall from the sky to burn the land and melt the stones. These are loathsome, inorganic monsters, unlike anything my species has imagined—but not so unlike what humans will one day build. At the time of my hatching, however, my species has no ability to comprehend what has befallen us. We can only fight.

The next fragment of memory comes from years later. I am charging from my hiding place to attack The Invaders. My brothers and sisters are beside me, so I fall back a little, allowing them to be the first to strike. Perhaps that terrifying explosion when I hatched taught me to be more cautious than the others. Perhaps some slight change in the threads of my essence granted me a greater sense of self-preservation. Whatever the case, I am rewarded for my restraint: although we can rip their limbs from their bodies, they burn us with invisible flames, and our bravest warriors perish faster than they can be hatched.

Another memory, two centuries later. I am in a counsel chamber deep under the earth, surrounded by distinguished members of my species. We are losing the war. The Invaders are few in number and sporadic in their attacks, but they have altered the chemistry of the air and the oceans. Other species are dying in droves—our herds, our pets, even the forests of ferns which shelter us are beginning to wither and disappear. If this continues, jellyfish will be the only animal life left on Earth.

The other members of the council present plans for altering our bodies to better adapt to our new environment. I slash the wall with my claws and announce that war is the only answer. For many long centuries we have been attempting to make our warriors larger and stronger, and I am the pinnacle of this effort. I now suggest that the answer lies not in the might of a few, but in the teeming of many. I have created a new disease, one that will feed upon the metal and crystal of The Invaders' bodies.

The other members of my species are petty, but they are not foolish. My plan is ratified. When next The Invaders appear, we do not attack openly. Instead, we hide in the tunnels nearby and let our animal thralls deliver our new weapon for us. I designed the bacteria to spread harmlessly at first so that it will increase exponentially before it becomes harmful. The Invaders will pass it among their kind before realizing it has infected them, and then it will be too late for them to fight.

By the next rainy season, we begin to see streaks of flame in the sky. Our enemies are dropping from the heavens. Some of my peers claim to have discovered charred and melted chunks of their bodies in the bottom of impact craters, but I never again see any trace of The Invaders.

Thirty thousand summers pass. I stand in the highest boughs of the only city our species has ever created or will ever create. Once, we built with metal and stone, but now we shape the trees themselves to form our homes. In the wake of the vanquishing, the war-time momentum of technological development has carried my species into a new era. Where once we used tools, now we create life to do our bidding. The power and the whims of my species are displayed in the streets below me: we have produced beasts of absurd size, or with ridiculous, bony plates on their backs, or any of a thousand other strange alterations. It is all for the sake of amusement or service.

The greatest modifications we reserve for ourselves, and most of my peers have transformed their bodies not for power or survival, but for pleasure. They spend summer and winter blissfully eating, rutting, and reveling, foolish in their newfound agelessness, and too short-sighted even to fix the genetic flaw that draws all of us to the same breeding grounds, like eels in the ocean. This is why, in all the world, we have but one city. This is why we could never hope to recover from the great falling rock that cast our planet into darkness.

Those who had built themselves for pleasure soon

died, along with all their living creations. Others, such as me, had built themselves for survival. With no need for each other, we wander our separate ways. I have not seen another of my species for seven million summers. Most likely, I am the only one left.

I never mourn the death of my cousins. Why should I? I need nothing from them, emotionally or physically. I can transform myself into any shape, adapt to any situation, and give rise to any living creature to serve my will. I need nothing from the ghosts of the past.

As I digest these memories, I find myself again. The real me, the one born only five summers ago, now lays on the rough stone floor of The Dragon's lair. I have forgotten how to move. I forget even how to breathe, until the pain in my ·lungs builds up and breaks through the dream.

"You have learned the history of our species," The Dragon's voice echoes in the darkness. "You have learned how our kind died off, until there was just me. And now you, who were made from the forgotten scraps of our discoveries."

"The humans," I say. "They must terrify you."

A slight pause before the answer. "Nothing terrifies me."

"But the humans are inventive, as we were. They may one day rival us. Surely they deserve respect, at least, for how far they've come."

"The humans are nothing," The Dragon says, an edge to his words. "I blinked, and they evolved. I will blink again, and they will be gone."

"What about their technology?" I ask. "Are you not afraid that their metal creations are so reminiscent of The Invaders—"

"I fear nothing!" The Dragon's roar hits me like a physical blow. Then, a wave of heat rushes over me. The Dragon, in his anger, has allowed all of his body heat to rush out of him at once. The rocks, the pool, everything in that cavern seems ablaze with reflected infrared light.

Now that I can see him clearly in his wrath, I am stunned by what I behold. His body is not unlike mine in its basic structure, but he is longer, more serpentine in shape, and even bigger than I imagined. His head is a massive, blazing mask of teeth and venom floating above me.

I cower. If I move, I might provoke his predatory instinct. After a time, the heat diminishes, and The Dragon pulls back slightly, just enough to let me know I may open my eyes. He no longer needs to hide from me.

"Humans are poisonous creatures," the words come in a huff of foul breath. "Poisonous, and tenacious. I have seen their herd attacked by diseases that should have obliterated them, but the humans display a strange kind of immunity that comes from outside their bodies. What is it? I do not understand how they resist extinction."

I must think for a moment before speaking, as much to gather my courage as to gather my thoughts.

"I think I know what you mean," I say. "Their science can cure that which is beyond their bodies' ability to heal. They call it 'medicine,' and it grants them many weapons against disease."

He grunts. "This resistance did not exist a few hundred summers ago. How is this possible?"

"Their progress is swift. Swifter than evolution."

The Dragon regards me quietly. His eyes make me feel like a mouse in an owl's talons.

"You have lived among them?" he asks slowly. "You understand their technology?"

"To some degree, yes," I answer.

"Do you wish to become one of them?"

Instead of responding, I look at my claws. So often, I have wished that I could exchange them for fingers—fingers to type on keyboards and turn doorknobs and, if I needed a weapon, to pick up a gun. These knives at the end of my hand, primitive weapons that they are, seem a poor substitute for all the wonders of human life.

"I can give you a human body," The Dragon says. "You could bring the human hatchling back to its mother and they would take you in as one of their own, because you would be just like them. I know you want this, and I can grant this wish."

"Why would you do such a thing for me?"

"Symbiosis," his voice sinks to a snake's hiss. "All I ask is that you tell me what you learn. Tell me how humans can be so weak as individuals yet so strong as a herd. Tell me how they live… and how they die."

I wrap my arms and tail around my knees and think. For most of my short life, I have been seeking in vain for one of my own kind to teach me about myself. Now that I have found The Dragon, I have the answer I do not want: I am a flawed prototype, engineered for a world that no longer exists. Two hundred million summers separates me from the companionship of my kind. I am not human, but if I become one of them, at least I would be something.

"Make me human," I say. "Make me one of their herd."

III. The Humans

"You wanna tell us how you found the kid?" The square-jawed male human plants his fists onto the table and leans heavily toward me. He wears a gray suit that is almost exactly the color that my skin used to be. Now, my skin is a very light brown, and it cannot shift into any other shade. I am human, at least on the surface.

"Well?" the man demands. "You gonna tell me about you and the kid?"

I stare. I have not yet mastered my new tongue and jaw, and I find responding with words to be extremely difficult. Even if I could form an intelligible answer, I'm not sure what to say. Yesterday, I was a reptile creature who snatched the child away from two armed humans. Last night I struck a bargain with a creature older than this continent and then entered a chrysalis that dissolved my flesh and bones and rebuilt them into a different body. This morning, I emerged from the sewers, naked, with a child in my arms.

I reach for the cup they have provided for me. My new fingers are surprisingly difficult to use, so I must lift the cup with both hands. Despite my care, some of the water dribbles down my chin. I look up to find the human leaning in close, his lips pulling back to reveal his teeth. Without my claws, I would have no way to defend myself against him.

"The kid," he says. "Talk."

I try. My words come out mushy, like a child's speech. The human tongue is such a tricky instrument.

"Quit playing dumb!" He knocks my cup off the table. "I got no patience for a kid-snatching monster like you—"

The door of the tiny room slams open. Another human in a different color suit beckons to the first, and they step out into the hall. With my weak human ears, I cannot hear all of their words, but I gather they are speaking about me. I catch the phrases "severe autism" and "escaped from his home" and "reported missing years ago." From this, I conclude that there was once a human who looked exactly like me, and they believe I am he. At least now I know where The Dragon gathered the DNA to create my new body.

The door opens, and the second human moves as if to step into the room, but the first man holds him back.

"Coulda sworn he understood me, though," The first human says. "If he's really such a basket case, then how'd he end up with a rich kid worth a million-dollar ransom?"

"Weirdest case ever," the second human shrugs. Then he proceeds into the room and sits down across from me. He does not smile, but he doesn't frown, either.

"Look," he says. "I don't know if you can understand me, but you obviously aren't capable of kidnapping anyone. Can you—can you at least tell me where you found the kid?"

I wait in patient silence. He waits in impatient silence.

"Earth to John Doe?" he waves his hand in front of my face. Then he sighs, and he stands up. "Listen, you're now officially free to go. Just sit here and I'll send someone to take you... wherever it is you belong."

He exits. The door does not click behind him. I consider his offer but decide that I do not belong anywhere, and therefore I do not need someone to take me there. Instead, I get up and walk out of the building.

I am always tempted to think of humans in the plural: *they* move, *they* build, *they* destroy. But now that I am one of them—at least in appearance—I am struck by how little they attend to one another. Now I see no *they* at all, but rather a collection of individuals who can barely coexist. On the sidewalk, humans walk swiftly, each turning their eyes from all others as if pretending they are the only ones present. A man in a dirty coat sits with his back against a brick wall, a ragged cardboard sign displayed in his lap. Most ignore him, and even the passers-by who drop coins and bills into his hat do not look at him or speak to him. Across the road, a recent collision has left two crumpled cars partially blocking the lane. It is impossible to determine if anyone was hurt or killed, but two males stand arguing next to the cars amid a ring of brightly burning road flares. I put my hand up to shield my eyes from the searing radiance of the flares, but the drivers of other cars do not acknowledge them except to honk in protest at the inconvenience of having to go around. One human's life-altering or life-ending event is nothing more than a nuisance to the others.

So weak as individuals yet so strong as a herd. That's how The Dragon described this species, but now it's difficult to see the strength.

"Hey, John Doe," A woman's voice pierces the sidewalk din. She sits in a car that has slid to the curb, and she is looking at me through her rolled-down window. "John Doe—if that's your real name—I just need a word."

I remember that the man in the police station called me John Doe. Evidently, that is my human name. I look through the car window and see a woman, not old and not young, leaning across her front passenger seat to speak to me.

"Listen," she says. "I just wanted to—okay, you should know something. That was my son you found. Or saved. Or whatever. And I'm not sure if I need to thank you or prosecute you, but—man, this is a weird situation. Would you mind just getting in? I just want to talk. At the very least, I owe you dinner or something."

The rear door of the car pops open, inviting me in. I catch a whiff of strong perfume. This might have nose-blinded me in my old body, but to my human nose it smells pleasantly of vanilla and several other flavors I do not recognize.

The scent makes my stomach growl with hunger, and the offer of a meal is attractive. Besides, I took on this human appearance to participate in the life of the human herd, and I cannot do that without participating in their communal eating behaviors. Therefore, I decide to accept her offer.

My legs are longer and less flexible than the ones I am accustomed to, but they are easier to use than fingers. I manage to enter the car with something that might resemble my former grace. The door closes automatically behind me and all the sounds of the street are instantly blocked away. The sudden silence is startling, and the perfume is just shy of overwhelming.

The steering wheel folds back into the dashboard and the driver's seat spins around so that the woman faces me.

"Nikola," she says.

"Yes, madam?" A voice answers, seemingly from nowhere.

"Drive to that steak house I like."

"Yes, madam."

I realize that she is speaking to the car itself. Then I see that the car is moving by itself, calmly and carefully steering us out into traffic while its only human occupant sits with her back to the road.

Humans cannot create living thralls as The Dragon does, but many of their machines serve just as effectively. I was once amused by these devices. Now that I have tasted the ancient memory of the mechanical invaders who once brought mass extinction to this planet, I am not so comfortable in their presence.

The woman fidgets with a large purse, her hand resting uneasily over the unzipped opening. I catch a glimpse of a perfume bottle and the chrome butt of a pistol inside the purse. Perhaps she meant for me to see the weapon as a display of power, just as a rattlesnake would shake its tail to warn away danger.

"Is that really your name?" she asks. "John Doe?"

I nod. It is as good a name as any.

"They tell me that you... you have trouble speaking. The police said you might not be able to understand me. But you can understand me just fine, can't you?"

I nod.

"My name is Lisa Baker. Do you know who I am?"

I shake my head.

"I'm the CEO of Moonshot Enterprises. You've heard of Moonshot, haven't you?"

I shake my head.

"The search engine? The self-driving cars? None of that rings any bells with you?" She seems to think this over. "Listen, John, you can't imagine what a strange week I've had. I don't think I even know who I am right now. To turn around and find my son gone, right in the middle of a crowded street. Then to see the news report with those pictures of what is either a guy in the world's greatest lizard costume, or else it really is an alien or a chupacabra like all the truthers are freaking out about—I'm confused, John. All I know is that he—it—the thing in the picture—was holding my son. My Connor."

She seems too confused for words for a moment. She places her hands on the side of her head, then she slides them forward, interlacing her fingers and staring at a point in space between the two of us.

I look at her and blink. The car accelerates onto a freeway onramp.

"I'm sorry," she says. "I just went half a week without sleeping. Can you just tell me—I just need to know. What happened? What happened with Connor and how did you find him?"

I attempt to say *I took him from the child thieves,* but it comes out sounding more like "Idooga fuma chilethees."

"You took him?" she echoes, seeming to understand me better than any other human so far. "Just like that? You took him—from a group of heavily armed thugs? Where are they now?"

"Dead," I say.

"Yes, one died in a car crash. And the others? What about them?"

"One other," I say, the words slurring a little less with practice. "Also dead… eaten."

"Eaten," she repeats. Her voice is quiet, probably because I have inadvertently triggered her instinctual fear of predators. "Eaten by that—that chupacabra thing?"

I don't know how to answer that question. Is The Dragon a "chupacabra thing" like me? Or is he something entirely different?

Lisa Baker gives me time to think, but eventually she breaks the silence by pressing a button on the dash panel. This triggers a small cargo compartment to slide out between my feet. It contains a black briefcase, which she gestures for me to take. My fingers struggle with the latches, but when the lid finally pops open I see bundles of green paper money.

"When my son disappeared, I went absolutely crazy," she says. "I called the cops, but in a fit of paranoia I started gathering cash, just in case there was a ransom. I tried to gather one million dollars in unmarked bills, just like they always ask for in movies. Like I said, I was going crazy. Anyway, I only managed to get seven hundred and eighty-nine thousand. You're holding it now, all the would-be ransom."

I run my fingers over the flat paper strips, so neatly stacked inside the case. Once, out of curiosity about why humans prize this green paper so much, I ate some. I detected only the bitter residue of the pigments and the hint of brightly stinging bleach. I still do not understand its value.

"There was a time when I would have cut off my own arm for that much money," Lisa Baker says. "After this last week—well, I've changed. I found out I was willing to give away everything I owned for my son. So, how about this deal: we forget lunch, you keep that briefcase, and we agree never to see each other again. Call it your reward. What do you say to that?"

I fold the lid closed and place the briefcase back in its drawer.

"No thank you," I say.

"Really?" Her eyes are large and her mouth hangs slightly open, suggesting she is experiencing the instinct of being startled. "You don't want the money?"

"Lunch is better," I say. "I am hungry."

She eyes me for another moment.

"You're serious, aren't you?"

I nod.

She looks out the window for a long time. Then she puts the purse with the gun on the seat next to her.

"Nikola," she says.

"Yes, madam?"

"New destination. Forget the restaurant and take us home. Also: order a drone to bring us a full steak meal. Three servings. We are going to have a special guest for dinner."

Lisa Baker offers me what food she has in the car, which consists of two long, processed meat sticks. This type of food is delightful because I can taste all sorts of animals inside the processed meat, including three different mammals and two different insects. The Dragon, it seems, allowed me to keep my ability to taste DNA.

The drive is long, perhaps two hours, and Lisa

Baker spends most it speaking to other humans via her car's communication system. I understand very little of what she is saying—much is about "investor confidence" and "the board of directors." I nod off, because having my skin and bones dissolved by enzymes and then rebuilt to resemble another species has proven to be a tiring experience.

When I awaken, I am hungrier than before. The sun is creeping down toward the horizon, layering the horizon in orange and pink. We have pulled off the main road and onto a long driveway that leads to a pair of fences, one inner and one outer, both of which automatically open to allow the car to pass. Clusters of cameras dot the walls every few dozen paces, and a crew of humans in blue overalls and yellow hats work together to string up cables between them. This must be Lisa Baker's home, and Lisa Baker must be in the process of upgrading its security.

I lived for a time on a college campus far to the north. It was cold but beautiful, with trees and lakes enough for all the students and still space left over for me to hide. Lisa Baker's dwelling reminds me of this campus, not only because it is nestled away inside a great expanse of delicately preserved wild lands, but also because it is almost as big as that campus. So much territory, and yet it houses only two people. This seems a strange dwelling for members of a gregarious species.

The car travels down a short road and around a large pond. We stop in front of a massive dwelling with an intricate roof line that sweeps down at dramatic angles. The walls consist of at least as much glass as brick, and the front steps are constructed of massive stone slabs. Like the gates at the far end of the driveway, the ornate wooden double doors of the entrance sense our approach and swing open to allow us inside.

Inside, the décor includes equal parts burnished steel and polished wood. The entrance foyer is irregular in shape, yet still consists of the lines and right angles that are the hallmark of nearly all human-made objects.

"Wait here," Lisa Baker tells me.

I wait. Minutes pass. I grow bored. I grow hungry.

She re-emerges, standing halfway inside the threshold that leads to a hallway. I can see that she has her hand on her purse, and I assume she still has the gun inside.

"Connor," she says, looking down into the hall. "There is someone here who wants to see you. Will you come out?"

I see the child's face cautiously emerge from behind the corner. After he studies me for a moment, he steps out into the hallway.

I cock my head. He cocks his head.

He smiles and extends his arms toward me just as he did on the night I rescued him. Somehow, he has recognized me despite my human skin.

He runs toward me, arms outstretched. Without thinking, I scoop him up and hold him. He is smiling, a huge grin that shows off two missing teeth and a lake of saliva around his tongue.

"I've never seen him react that way to anyone before," Lisa Baker says. She seems to be relaxing as she speaks, and only now does she move her hand away from her purse. It seems that I have passed her test.

Connor wriggles out of my grasp, seizes my hand, and begins pulling me down the hallway.

"I think he wants to show you something," Lisa Baker says.

I follow. Connor knows the switchbacks and detours of this labyrinthine house. He bursts excitedly through a door to reveal what can only be his bedroom. Here, the walls are covered in posters of dragons, chameleons, monitor lizards, and even a few snakes. Connor ignores all that and takes me to a large glass enclosure at the back. Inside this enclosure, an iguana rests on a small log, holding his chest upward proudly as he warms himself beneath a heating lamp. The frills along his head and at his elbows give him a striking resemblance to my original body.

"Rex," Connor says, jamming his finger against the iguana's glass cage.

"Rex?" I repeat.

"It's the name of his iguana," Lisa Baker says. "I don't know why he loves lizards so much, but he always has. Disgusting creatures, if you ask me."

I look at her and remember to imitate a human smile.

"How old is Connor?" I ask.

"Five," she tells me.

Five summers. The same age as me. My knowledge of the human life cycle is limited, but it seems impractical for a species to require five whole years to develop into adulthood, and yet this child seems nowhere close to maturity.

Lisa Baker's wrist band buzzes and she glances at the message it displays.

"Dinner has just been loaded onto the drone," she says. "It should be here in about twenty-five minutes. Connor, do you want to go look at the balloons?"

Connor emits a wordless squeal of delight. He holds both of our hands and pulls us back into the hallway and outside to a massive courtyard. There is a fountain in the center of the courtyard and four large stone boxes spaced evenly around it. All the rest is green lawn carefully raised in the human style, with all plants other than grass having been ruthlessly exterminated. Lisa Baker must have diverted massive amounts of water to keep this lawn green in the middle of the desert.

Lisa Baker's fingers slide over her phone. The

instant she is finished, the four large stone boxes open, and from each unfurls an undulating mass of fabric that is at least as large in diameter as a human is tall. The fabric ripples and flaps as it fills with helium, and soon each of these balloons resolves itself into a flattened oval.

Connor watches in breathless anticipation. I look to Lisa Baker because I do not know what to expect.

"If you've been reading about tech and industry, you might have heard about this," Lisa Baker says to me. "You're looking at Project Stratosphere, which some call Moonshot Enterprise's most ambitious endeavor. Others call it a foolish waste of company resources. I've been printing out all the headlines, good and bad. Someday I'm going to make a scrap book."

She seems to grow with pride, inflating like one of her balloons. Behind her, the sky fades to dusky blue.

When the balloons reach their full size, they rise from their beds to hover in the air just a little higher than my fingers can reach. Suddenly, scintillating colors burst to life along their sides, sliding up and down the entire spectrum of light that is visible to the human eye. Sometimes the colors mingle in great, random swirls, and at other times they resolve themselves into spirals of red, yellow, and green with wheels of blue at the center. In the dim light, these balloons are mesmerizing, like creatures from the deepest seas come to explore our world. Connor runs back and forth across the lawn, chasing the floating light shows wherever they drift.

As a balloon glides in toward me, I gather myself to jump toward it, but a stinging pain slices through both of my knees. I straighten myself so that I do not fall over. I do not understand why my joints hurt in this way.

Lisa Baker does not notice my sudden pain.

"Project Stratosphere isn't just pretty lights," she says to me. "We are going to launch almost two million of these over the next seven years. They're solar powered, capable of staying aloft for years without maintenance, and each will provide internet service for thousands of people in developing countries who might not otherwise have access. Within the decade, every human being on Earth will be a connected member of the information age."

"Every human being connected?" As I repeat her words, I look at the windows of the house. All is dark. All is quiet. I am confused by the human drive to "connect" with people from the other side of the world while at the same time building fences to remain isolated from those closest at hand.

Lisa Baker watches her son chase the balloons. I watch her. Humans are always speaking, yet I have noticed they usually say the least important thing first. If you don't give them time, they rarely say anything worthwhile.

"You know, it's funny," she continues in a distant tone. "When I started this project, I thought of the five billion people in unindustrialized countries as nothing more than potential customers. Now, after this last week… my perspective is changing. Those are five billion human beings who get to emerge from the darkness of history. Five billion minds who get to join in the global conversation. I'm—look at me, will you?" she wipes her eyes with the back of her hand. "My employees sometimes call me the ice queen when they think I can't hear them. Doesn't take much to melt the ice, I guess. Listen—I have to go to the hangar tomorrow. That's where we're keeping all our balloons in preparation for the big launch day next month. How would you like a tour of the factory?"

"Yes, I would like that," I say.

Her wrist band buzzes. She glances at a message.

"Dinner's here," she says to me. Then she calls to Connor.

My knees still tingle with pain and now I find that my ankles hurt as well. I move slowly and am the last to enter the house. Just before I go inside, I glance back, expecting to absorb one more glimpse of the flying lights. Instead, my gaze is drawn to the high peak of the roof, where I see the silhouette of a buzzard hunched against the darkening sky.

Buzzards are not nocturnal creatures. This one has come to me from The Dragon.

I retreat indoors. We eat. Lisa Baker guides Connor to bed and tells me to sleep in the guest room on the opposite side of the house. I am happy to rest, because the pain in my legs persists, and now my shoulders hurt as well. Perhaps this is normal for humans, but I do not think so. It seems more likely that there is some flaw in the body The Dragon gave me. At least my fingers still easily work the doorknob of my room, and this gives me a feeling of freedom and power that is well worth a little discomfort.

Before I can lie down, there is a tapping at my window. It is the buzzard I saw on the roof.

His tapping becomes so insistent that I must open the window before he breaks the glass.

"The Dragon speaks through me," the buzzard recites. "He issues a command."

"I do not take commands from The Dragon," I say. "That was not our bargain."

In reply, the buzzard extends his foot, showing that he has something clutched within his talons. I extend my hand to accept a clump of fungus. It is the size of a chicken egg, but composed of irregular pustule-like sacks. The color is brownish-green.

"What is it?" I ask.

"The Dragon wishes you to know that it will not hurt you," the buzzard says. "It is capable only of exterminating human civilization."

"Is that all?" I ask.

Impulsively, I lift the spoor to my mouth and lick it. I taste a disease, but not a disease that can infect me— the buzzard spoke the truth about that. In fact, it will not directly harm any living creature. Contained within the pustules of the fungus are colonies of bacteria that will quietly and slowly breed for years. Then—I taste this clearly in their genetic code—they will multiply with sudden aggression, and switch their metabolic wastes to a compound that will dissolve both silicone and copper. Silicone and copper are the essential ingredients of human technology, which means that this bacteria, if allowed to spread, could potentially destroy computers, cell phones, and power lines.

"This is the bio-weapon," I say in amazement. "This is a variation on the weapon that The Dragon used to destroy The Invaders back in the ancient era."

The buzzard twists his skull-like face toward me but does not reply. He has no preprogrammed response, so he remains silent. In many ways, The Dragon's thralls are as mindless as the humans' machines.

"What does The Dragon wish me to do with this disease?" I ask.

"The Dragon commands you to release the disease when you visit the breeding ground of the floating things."

It takes me a moment to work out that "breeding ground of the floating things" means "factory for the stratosphere balloons." The buzzard must have overheard Lisa Baker offering to take me to the factory tomorrow.

I cannot help but utter a very human laugh.

"This weapon will not work against humans," I say.

"Unlike The Invaders, the humans have a very clear concept of diseases. They will know how to fight it. Within a few years, they will develop poisons that will kill off these tiny creatures."

"The Dragon wishes you to know that he has come to a new understanding of human capability, thanks to absorbing your memories."

That stops my humor. A creeping coldness spreads from my stomach toward my heart.

"My memories?"

"The Dragon replicated and tasted all of your memories while you were in the chrysalis. He now knows everything you have ever known about the humans, and he has used that knowledge to formulate his strategy."

The shock of this revelation, combined with the growing pain in my knees, causes me to lose my balance. I sit down heavily on the floor. To say that I feel violated is an understatement. The Dragon has read my memory—he has consumed everything I have ever been, the way the ocean consumes a single raindrop. Yes, I chose to entrust my life to The Dragon, expecting full well that he might betray me by killing me. Instead, he used my foolishness as a weapon not against me, but against the human species.

"When the floating things go into the sky, they will be infected," the buzzard, oblivious to my shock, continues his speech. "Then, a mere few summers hence, the disease will become active and will not only consume the floating things, it will rain down from them, spread by the winds across the human-infested planet, infecting and destroying all of their machines."

Now there is no question in my mind that The Dragon's plan will work. Lisa Baker's balloons will serve as both incubator and distribution vector for the extinction of human technology. Once reaching the point of virulence aboard the balloons, the disease will spill from it to pervade the atmosphere. It will appear everywhere at once, falling to Earth in such a wide-spread assault that the humans would not have time to develop their defenses, especially as the very tools they might use to combat it crumble in their fingers. Without their cars, computers, electricity, or communications, human civilization would disintegrate. Even though the metal-eating disease would not harm their bodies, they would soon succumb to mass famine and bloody war. After that, perhaps The Dragon would choose to reveal himself and rule them as a god. Or perhaps he would simply feast upon the creatures he had made helpless. Maybe some of both.

"There will be piles of human carrion to feast upon." The buzzard croaks. "*Piles* of carrion."

He makes a scissoring sound with his beak and settles his head smugly against his body. Perhaps he can understand the message that he delivers after all, because he seems to relish the idea.

I care not for The Dragon's commands, but I must still consider whether I should release this disease. True, a few humans have been kind to me, but far more have been cruel. Even to themselves, their cruelty often seems to outweigh their kindness, and they give so little thought to how they trample other animals in their march toward what they call progress. Their own scientists have noted that they are killing species as fast as the climate change that followed the great meteor sixty-five million summers ago. Then, the dinosaurs were wiped out by a random cosmic event. Now, bees, tigers, manatees and more are disappearing, all eliminated by callous species-ism.

I stare at the spoor cluster in my hand. It weighs virtually nothing, yet my wrist and shoulder ache as I hold it. It is the burden of holding the doom of all humanity in my palm. If I release this disease, millions of humans will die. If I do not, millions of species will fall into extinction. The question is really one of loyalty: am I loyal to human life, or am I loyal to all other life?

"The Dragon wishes to ensure your cooperation," the buzzard says, as if his master had been able to anticipate my dilemma. "You have been experiencing pain, starting in your joints. The suffering is because The Dragon changed your outward shape but not your internal life essence. Your body is still growing according to its original pattern, which is not compatible with your current shape. There will be agony. You will not survive the transformation back to your true self without The Dragon's assistance."

I know he is speaking the truth. It is not just the pain that confirms it: I cannot escape my true nature. My knees, hips, shoulders, and elbows all suddenly seem to burn more intensely, as if the flames of agony have been fanned by the buzzard's words.

"What does The Dragon want of me?" I ask.

"When you have placed the disease, The Dragon will welcome you back and will allow you to use the chrysalis he has already prepared for you. This new chrysalis will allow you to safely revert to your original body which, no doubt, you now realize is far superior to the shape you currently wear. And to ensure the cooperation of the human female, The Dragon has taken the child that she—and you—seem so strangely protective of."

Those beady black eyes seem to bore into me. A thrall is not capable of untruth, so I know he is not bluffing.

I lunge from the floor, ignoring the pain in my legs, and stumble through the house until I find the Connor's bedroom. The door is locked, so I kick it open. Splinters of wood spray from the latch as it breaks.

Connor's bed is empty, the sheets shoved to the side. The window nearest to him is open, curtains blowing in the cool night wind.

Lisa Baker has set up a bed so that she could sleep in the room with her child. I shake her in an attempt to wake her, but she continues to sleep. I yell to her that the agents of The Dragon have taken her son. She does not answer. She is breathing, but her eyes remain closed. A small red bump on the side of her neck tells me why. The Dragon must have sent one of his insect thralls to sting her with the sleeping venom. She is not dead because The Dragon needs her for his plan, but she will not awaken for many hours.

I sink to the floor. Whatever I do next, I cannot escape with my life: if I obey The Dragon, he may kill me at his whim. If I do not, I will die painfully as my body tries to regrow into its original form. The only remaining question is how I want to end. Shall I be complicit in the murder of seven billion human beings and then die swiftly in The Dragon's jaws, or shall I protect a genocidal species by allowing myself to die slowly and painfully?

I sit in that room between the sleeping human and the watchful gaze of the caged iguana. Humans are not my species. Therefore, I know the rational choice is the one that grants the greatest chance of survival. But when I look at Connor's empty bed, surrounded by posters of reptiles, I realize have already made the irrational decision.

What I would not do for seven billion human beings, I will do for a single person.

IV. The Extinction

Almost everything I need is in Lisa Baker's purse. She has perfume, a pistol, and the key fob that prompts the car to unlock its doors and turn on its engine.

"Nikola," I say when I am seated.

"Yes, madam?" the car responds obediently, evidently unable to distinguish my voice from that of its master. Sometimes, tricking human technology is as easy as drawing ants to sugar.

I recite the address of the house where I first rescued Connor from the child-thieves. It was easy to find this information, because I have seen humans use their phones often enough. In Lisa Baker's phone, I found many recent postings, including countless blurry photographs of me—the true me—holding the child on the street. For the first time, I understand how I must appear to the human herd. In those photographs, I am an alien thing wrapped in shadows, attempting to abduct a vulnerable child for unclear purposes. I am saddened to see myself this way, but it does not change my mind.

While the car proceeds along the highway, I fold down the back seat to access the trunk. I discover road flares and stuff them into the purse. Then, I recline in the seat and allow myself to writhe in the agony for a short time.

With each passing hour, the pain increases inside my body. I can feel my dorsal quills scraping the inside of my skin. My joints click when I move because the bones are no longer perfectly aligned. My fingers, my wonderful, miraculous fingers, hurt worst of all. The beds of my fingernails bleed because my claws are re-growing and will soon burst free. At that moment when I am caught half way between two different species, I will die.

Despite the pain, I begin to wonder what Lisa Baker will think when she awakens. She will find her son missing, the door to his room broken open, and her car and purse stolen. She will conclude that John Doe, a man she trusted despite his strangeness, has taken her child. I am unsettled by the thought that she might think ill of me, despite the fact that John Doe, the version of me she will blame, will never exist again. Perhaps it is better to be forgotten than hated. In a way, I will be both.

The car carries me to the house where I first found Connor, but no amount of coaxing will convince it to depart the smooth human-built road to travel into the desert. That means I must cross the scrub lands on foot. Each step feels like a spear impaling my leg. I sweat profusely under the sun, and my tender human skin turns red and blisters. Twice I stumble, the pain of each fall multiplied a thousand times by my physical deterioration.

At least my memory remains clear: I know right

where the child-thief buried his incendiary chemicals. I must dig them up with my hands, a painful and slow process without claws, but I need what is in that bag.

Filthy, agonized, and with a dangerously overheated body, I sling the duffel bag over my shoulder and stumble forward to the next rise. There awaits the narrow tunnel and The Dragon's buzzard thrall.

"I speak for The Dragon," the buzzard croaks. "The Dragon wishes to know if you have finished your task—"

My answer comes in the form of a swift kick. The buzzard is a large bird, but its hollow bones make it flimsy compared to my simian solidity. When my foot strikes it, the bird simply disappears in a cloud of feathers. I do not look back to see where the buzzard lands or if it still breathes. Instead, I turn my head toward a glint in the sand. It is the human's knife, which he must have dropped here when The Dragon's thralls killed him.

I slide the knife into Lisa Baker's purse, next to the road flares. Then I lower myself onto my belly and push the duffel bag before me as I crawl down into the blackness.

After much effort and discomfort, I emerge into the cavern complex. The Dragon's thralls scuttle all around me. They ignore me, and I ignore them. I try to keep myself stable on my feet as I move toward The Dragon's inner sanctum. My eyesight is beginning to cloud over, but here it is so dark that no human eyes could see anything anyway.

I feel a sharp drop in the floor and know that I am standing in a trench which runs outside the inner sanctum. I am drawing closer. I drop the still-unzipped duffel bag into the trench and carry the purse by its straps. Then I proceed to grope my way along the wall like the blind man I am.

I travel many paces before The Dragon's voice stops me.

"What is the meaning of this?" the words boom from the shadows. "I can smell that you still have the disease spore with you. Why have you not infected the human machines?"

"I will not obey you," my voice is strained but defiant. "You will return the human child to me, or I will destroy you."

"Destroy me?" He roars. "Destroy *me*? With that pitiful little knife you carry in that sack?"

"Not the knife at first," I say. "I will begin with this." I light a road flare and suddenly the cavern is ablaze in vermilion brilliance. The light reveals The Dragon looming before me. He seems even larger than before, a prehistoric crocodile arising from the river of my own nightmares.

For all his size, however, he recoils from me, blinking. He is now partially blind, I know, because he made the mistake of looking directly at the flare. This may be the first bright light he's seen for millennia.

"I will chew your bones and then find another to spread the disease," The Dragon's voice shakes the ground. "But first you will watch me dine upon the human child you seem so ready to die for."

The massive jaws swing away from me and I see teeth glinting in the red light. He slithers more than walks, moving his great bulk on four short limbs toward a corner of the cave, not far from the memory pool. I see Connor in that corner, curled up and evidently sleeping soundly, no doubt having been subjected to the sleeping venom once more.

I throw the road flare down and draw the pistol from Lisa Baker's purse. I fire all six of its bullets as quickly as I can. Perhaps some of them strike The Dragon, perhaps some miss—it does not matter. Even if all six lead slugs pierced his brain or his heart, the beast is too massive to suffer more than a moment's irritation. What is more important is the sound of the gunfire. Inside the enclosed cavern, the noise strikes us both like a succession of hammer blows. Even my insensitive human ears are deafened. The Dragon's ears, which can detect the steps of tiny creatures far overhead, must now ring with unendurable pain.

The Dragon's eyes turn back to me. I now have his full, deadly attention.

It is true that The Dragon possesses all of my

memories, but it seems that he did not learn enough about me to guess that I might oppose him. Perhaps this is because he understands only the survival instinct, and I have acted in direct opposition that instinct. I, on the other hand, know exactly what he will do. Survival is rooted in fear, and fear becomes anger. I have made The Dragon angry. He knows that I am an inferior being, weak and frail, and that if I hurt him, he need only indulge his impulse to crush me. So, as predictable as one of the humans' machines, The Dragon abandons Connor and charges toward me.

I run.

Behind me, The Dragon shatters stalactites as he builds up speed. I feel stone chips bounce against my back, but I am able to dive through the tiny opening into the tunnel complex.

My joints blaze with agony. I have just enough time to light the second flare.

The Dragon slams into the wall, disintegrating it into a cloud of dirt and dust. The shockwave jolts my body and causes me to drop the flare. I must leave it where it falls.

I can feel the vibrations in the floor and walls as The Dragon's heavy footsteps thunder closer and closer. Fumblingly, I draw the glass vial of perfume from Lisa Baker's purse and slam it to the stony floor. It shatters, flooding the tunnel with sparkling chemical scents that assault my nose. For just a brief instant, I hear The Dragon's stride falter, and I know he must now be completely nose-blind.

I round the corner while lighting the third and final flare. I fling it as far down the tunnel as I can. As the flare leaves my hand, I hear a snap in my ankle. I tumble, managing only to roll into the trench on top of the duffel bag of explosive chemicals I left there.

I am crippled: I can run no farther. The Dragon will be around the corner and on top of me in a few heartbeats. All I can do now is find the ignition timer inside the duffel bag. It is pre-set for fifteen seconds, so I press the button to start the countdown. Then I draw my knife.

He comes around the corner, thundering like a herd of bulls. As each of his feet slams into the ground, I bounce a little in my place. But he is at least partially blind from the flares, deaf from the gunshots, and stripped of his olfactory sense by the perfume. He thrusts through the tunnel in pursuit of the flare that I threw ahead of me, because that is all he can perceive at the moment. Before he realizes where I am hiding, he is charging right above me.

With all the strength in my pitiful human arms, I thrust the knife up into his belly as he passes. His momentum almost rips the weapon out of my hands, but I squeeze my fingers tight and brace myself against the side of the trench, driving the blade deeper and deeper into him. Hot blood spills down over me and I feel The Dragon tensing, attempting to halt his momentum. I have created an incision no less than three feet in length. To The Dragon, this is not much more than a deep scratch, although a painful one.

He shudders and jerks away, but the tunnel prevents him from moving far. That's when I grab the duffel bag and jam it into the cut I have made. Blood makes my hands slippery, but I thrust with all my might to push it deep inside him before I scramble out of the trench and crawl back the way I came.

I try to stand but my ankle gives out beneath me. As I fall, I twist so that I can see The Dragon. He is so large that he has trouble turning inside his own tunnel, but what he lacks in maneuverability he makes up for with physical might. His claws rip out huge sections of the stony walls while simultaneously pulling his upper body back around, until he faces me. I feel as though I am falling into the two-hundred-million-year void that exists behind those red eyes.

Then, the chemicals inside the duffel bag ignite.

First, a white-hot ball appears inside his belly. This quickly spreads like veins of lava. The Dragon looks back at himself, watching for the single instant it takes the flames to eat him from within. Then he turns to look at me and opens his jaws. If he means to say something, he does not have time. Instead, he vomits a river of fire, and then more liquid heat spills from his nose, and then from his eyes. He is consumed by a bonfire that burns from the inside out. For a moment, his skull and his bones are dark shadows lit from behind, and then they, too, disappear in the orange and white inferno.

I raise my hand to shield my eyes from the light and the heat. The liquid flames ooze downhill, toward me, and I must crawl quickly to escape. I pause only long enough to fling the pustule sack that carried The Dragon's disease back into the fire.

All around me, The Dragon's thralls rush about in confusion. Many of the rats are aflame, scuttling like living torches and spreading the fire to others of their kind. By the time I return to The Dragon's inner lair, a stampede of burning animals are trampling each other on the way to hurling themselves into the memory pool. They are following some survival instinct that The Dragon allowed them to keep, but there are too many of them, and rather than extinguishing themselves they transform the pool into a lake of fire.

I find Connor, still in his venom-induced coma, and begin to drag him away. I find myself unable to fully close my right hand, so I hook my fingers into the collar of his shirt to get a better grip. The flames are spreading quickly. With my broken ankle and other injuries, I fear I might not be able to drag Connor to safety, let alone myself.

I stop and look in amazement toward the wall, where The Dragon has hung something. It is a large, flattened oval, withered like a deflated balloon and lined with dark, bark-like skin. This is a chrysalis, identical to the one which transformed me into a human. Could The Dragon have created it to transform me back? The Dragon's messenger had said this chrysalis had already been created, even though I had not dared hope it was true.

A thin voice of hope whispers to me: The Dragon might have lacked the ability to lie. Humans make deception seem so easy and commonplace that I forget it was an alien concept to my ancestors. I know The Dragon was capable of changing his mind and concealing truths, but he never showed the power to fabricate untruths. In order for him to say he created a new chrysalis for me, he may have needed to actually create a chrysalis.

Whatever the truth, I must move quickly. I tug the chrysalis from its perch and lay Connor on top of it, then use it to drag him through the tunnel. This allows me to carry him somewhat faster than I could without it. By the time we exit the cavern complex into the sewers, we are safely far enough away from the orange flames. I collapse onto the ground. For several minutes, even the process of breathing proves laborious and uncertain.

Connor is still in his coma. He will be safely asleep

for some time to come. With the last of my strength, I crawl inside the chrysalis. It seals itself behind me like the mouth of a carnivorous plant, and then I am lost in the sensation of floating on an ocean of warm, salty tears.

V. The Connection

A day later, I emerged from the chrysalis, restored to my original shape. My senses are sharp, my body is nimble and strong, and my skin can shift colors at my whim. I also have my claws again. I stare at them and wiggle them as much as they will move. They seem so inflexible and clumsy.

Connor is still asleep, though he looks thin and gaunt. The sleeping venom may slow his metabolism, but he has spent much of the past few days without proper food. He needs the care of his own kind. He needs his mother.

I scoop him up and travel toward his home as fast as the sewer-ways and backyards can take me. My re-transformation took almost a full day, so it is nighttime now, and I can easily move without being seen.

Along the way, I have too much time to think. The flames that I started consumed the memory pool, thereby destroying two hundred million years of knowledge. Its destruction was surely the greatest possible crime against science, and against life, and against my own species. I am haunted by the possibility that, if I could have drunk from that pool, I might have learned to transform my own body at my whim, just as The Dragon could. Now, that possibility is lost forever. Even if I survive this planet's next five extinction events, I will still feel the loss as a wound in my soul.

As we finally approach Connor's dwelling, he stirs in my arms. It is all I can do to keep him quiet as we scale the wall and slip past the cameras surrounding his house.

I climb the walls and peer through windows until I find Lisa Baker. She is sitting in her second-story bedroom. The room is dark, at least by human standards. She remains very still, her body hunched and her hands pressed against her face.

I tap gently at the window. She looks up. I hold Connor so that she can see him, and, I hope, so she can also see that I do not mean to harm him. For his part, Connor offers a groggy, half-toothed smile.

Her body language makes it clear that she is caught between two instincts: fear and love. Should she flee from this monster at her window, or should she run to her son? It takes almost no time for her to decide.

She opens the window, snatches Connor in her arms, and backs up several paces. She does not speak: she only looks deeply at my eyes as she holds her son. Does she recognize me as John Doe? I cannot see how—my true eyes look nothing like my human eyes did. Still, I let her study me, longer than I've let almost any human look before.

Allowing her this view could mean my death. If she decides I am to blame for her son's danger, she may use her vast wealth and powerful machines to hunt me down. I cannot say it would be entirely unjust: I may have been the one who rescued her son from The Dragon's den, but I was also the one who first carried him into it.

Hatred, however, isn't the only possible response. Perhaps, if she looks at me for long enough, I will no longer be alien to her. I have learned that humans possess the strange ability to trick their own instincts into accepting any creature as a member of their family group. Usually, this is an unconscious decision, but they do have the power to decide whether they see similarities or differences. They cannot eliminate their family-herd instinct, but they can consciously redirect it to include new people and creatures—if they choose to do so. I have determined that it is this strange, misguided, wonderful family instinct which leads them to be kind and to be cruel.

Lisa Baker is a human, which means she is conflicted. She is alone, connected, frightened, relieved, weak, and powerful all at the same time. She speaks of the importance of communicating with five billion humans on the other side of the planet, yet she has shielded herself from contact even from those who prepare her meals and protect her family. She looks at me and doesn't know if she sees a monster or a friend. I only wish I still had a human tongue to tell her that I am both.

I cock my head and watch a tear slide down her cheek. Then I step away, knowing it is time for me to fade into the dark summer's night.

Other Books by the Authors

All Four
Merely This and Nothing More: Poe Goes Punk
Unnatural Dragons

Lindsay Schopfer
The Adventures of Keltin Moore
Steampunk Adventure
The Beast Hunter
Into the North (coming winter 2016)

Survival Science Fiction
Lost Under Two Moons

Fantasy Anthology
Magic, Mystery, and Mirth

Jeffrey Cook
YA Scifi/Mystery
Mina Cortez: From Bouquets to Bullets

Dawn of Steam
Epistolary Steampunk
First Light
Gods of the Sun
Rising Suns

The Angels Grace Trilogy
Urban Fantasy
with AJ Downey
Airs & Graces
There But for the Grace
A Coup de Grace
(coming Winter 2016)

The Fair Folk Chronicles
YA Urban Fantasy
with Katherine Perkins
Foul is Fair
Street Fair
A Fair Fight
All's Fair

Nonfiction
with Lee French
Working the Table: An Indie Author's Guide to
Conventions

Anthology Appearances
Steampunk Trails #2

Asylum

Sound & Fury: Shakespeare Goes Punk

Once More Unto the Breach: Shakespeare Goes Punk 2

Lee French

The Maze Beset Trilogy
Superheroes In Denim

Dragons In Pieces

Dragons In Chains

Dragons In Flight

Spirit Knights
YA Urban Paranormal Adventure

Girls Can't Be Knights

Backyard Dragons

Ethereal Entanglements

Ghost Is the New Normal (coming 2017)

In the Ilauris setting
Standalone Fantasy tales

Damsel In Distress

Shadow & Spice (short story)

Al-Kabar

The Greatest Sin
Epic Fantasy co-authored with Erik Kort
The Fallen
Harbinger
Moon Shades
Illusive Echoes

Anthology Appearances
Into the Woods: a fantasy anthology
Missing Pieces VIII (coming August 2016)
Artifact
(coming November 2016)

Nonfiction
with Jeffrey Cook
Working the Table: An Indie Author's Guide to
Conventions

Sechin Tower
The Mad Science Institute Trilogy
Young Adult Teslapunk
Mad Science Institute
The Non-Zombie Apocalypse
Ghost Storm

Made in the USA
Columbia, SC
17 August 2018